Praise for *Fatal Forgery*

"I loved the sense of place, with some surprising revelations about jail and courthouse conditions and operations, and an interesting change of setting at one point, which I won't reveal for fear of spoiling the plot. There was great attention to detail woven skilfully into the writing, so I felt I learned a lot about the era by osmosis, rather than having it thrust upon me. All in all, a remarkable debut novel."

Debbie Young, author and book blogger

"From the start of this story I felt as if I had been transported back in time to Regency London. Walking in Sam's footsteps, I could hear the same cacophony of sound, shared the same sense of disbelief at Fauntleroy's modus operandi, and hung onto Constable Plank's coat tails as he entered the squalid house of correction at Coldbath Fields. I am reassured that this is not the last we shall see of Samuel Plank. His steadfastness is so congenial that to spend time in his company in future books is a treat worth savouring."

Jo at Jaffareadstoo

Praise for *The Man in the Canary Waistcoat*

"Having read the first Sam Plank novel and really enjoyed it I was so looking forward to the next, and 'The Man in the Canary Waistcoat' did not disappoint. Susan Grossey is an excellent storyteller. The descriptions of Regency London are vivid and create a real sense of time and place. Sam Plank, Martha and Wilson are great characters – well-drawn and totally individual in their creation. The dialogue is believable and the pace well fitted to this genre. The novel shows excellent research and writing ability – a recommended read."

Barbara Goldie, The Kindle Book Review

"Regency police constable Sam Plank, so well established in the first book, continues to develop here, with an interesting back story emerging about his boyhood, which shapes his attitude to crime as an adult. Like the first book, this is not so much a whodunit as a whydunit, and Grossey skilfully unfolds a complex tale of financial crime and corruption. There are fascinating details about daily life in the criminal world woven into the story, leaving the reader much more knowledgeable without feeling that he's had a history lesson."

Debbie Young, author and book blogger

Praise for *Worm in the Blossom*

"Ever since I was introduced to Constable Sam Plank and his intrepid wife Martha, I have followed his exploits with great interest. There is something so entirely dependable about Sam: to walk in his footsteps through nineteenth century London is rather like being in possession of a superior time travelling machine... The writing is, as ever, crisp and clear, no superfluous waffle, just good old fashioned storytelling, with a tantalising beginning, an adventurous middle, and a wonderfully dramatic ending."

Jo at Jaffareadstoo

"Susan Grossey not only paints a meticulous portrait of London in this era, she also makes the reader see it on its own terms, for example recognising which style of carriage is the equivalent to a 21st century sports-car, and what possessing one would say about its owner... In short, a very satisfying and agreeable read in an addictive series that would make a terrific Sunday evening television drama series."

Debbie Young, author and book blogger

Praise for *Portraits of Pretence*

"There is no doubt that the author has created a plausible and comprehensive Regency world and with each successive novel I feel as if I am returning into the bosom of a well-loved family. Sam and Martha's thoughtful care and supervision of the ever-vulnerable Constable Wilson, and of course, Martha's marvellous ability, in moments of extreme worry, to be her husband's still small voice of calm is, as always, written with such thoughtful attention to detail. As one book finishes I am heartened to know that, like buses, another one will be along soon; after all, the author did say that there would be seven Sam Plank stories and I am holding her to that promise."

Jo at Jaffareadstoo

"Do you want to know what a puff guts is or a square toes or how you would feel if you were jug-bitten? Well, you'll find out in this beautifully researched and written Regency crime novel. And best of all you will be in the good company of Constable Sam Plank, his wife Martha and his assistant Constable Wilson. These books have immense charm and it comes from the tenderness of the depiction of Sam's marriage and his own decency. The plot revolves around revolution, murders and the trade in miniatures and there are some fascinating descriptions of Custom House."

Victoria Blake, author

FAITH, HOPE AND TRICKERY

Susan Grossey

Susan Grossey
Publisher

Copyright © 2018 by Susan Grossey

All rights reserved. No part of this publication may be reproduced, distributed or transmitted in any form or by any means, including photocopying, recording, or other electronic or mechanical methods, without the prior written permission of the author, except in the case of brief quotations embodied in critical reviews and certain other non-commercial uses permitted by copyright law.

This novel is a work of fiction. The events and characters in it, while based on real historical events and characters, are the work of the author's imagination.

Book layout ©2018 BookDesignTemplates.com

Portraits of Pretence / Susan Grossey -- 1st edition
ISBN 978-1-9160019-4-7

For Richard Reynolds,
with gratitude for his support, encouragement,
wise words, and shelf-space

Men willingly believe what they wish to be true.

—JULIUS CAESAR

Author's note

Any period of history has its own vocabulary, both standard and slang. The Regency was no different, and in order to capture the spirit of the time I have used words and phrases that may not be familiar to the modern reader. At the end of this book there is a glossary of these terms and their brief definitions.

CHAPTER ONE

The leather cutter's wife

FRIDAY 4TH JULY 1828

The man sitting on the bench against the wall in the front office of Great Marlborough Street police office looked familiar, and indeed he stood as I walked in, as though he had been waiting for me. I looked questioningly at Tom Neale, the office-keeper, in his usual place behind the counter.

"One for you, Sam," Tom said, nodding at the visitor. "I have offered him the pick of the constables to help with his business – even our young Mr Wilson – but he says that he will speak only to you." He leaned towards me and lowered his voice. "Shook up, I would say he is. He's given me no trouble, and he's polite enough, but definitely shook up."

I turned to the man, and recollected that I did know him. "Mr Humphries, isn't it?" I said. "The bootmaker, from Conduit Street?"

He nodded. "You have an excellent memory, Constable Plank – it must be, what, nearly three years now. But then I suppose an ability to recall faces is as important to you as knowledge of a person's feet is to me."

I thought back to when I had last seen Humphries. "Is this to do with Mr Macintosh?" I asked.

The bootmaker shook his head. "No, thank heavens. I am thankful to say that I have heard no more from him; mind you, I am a deal more cautious these days, about my business associates."

I waited, but he said no more. "In that case, Mr Humphries, what is it I can do for you today?"

Humphries looked over my shoulder towards Tom's counter and the door. "Would it be possible to speak somewhere more private, constable?"

"Is the back office free, Tom?" I asked.

The office-keeper nodded. "Constable Wilson has gone out in search of his second breakfast, and all other constables are attending warrants." He glanced past me at Humphries. "Tea is in order, I think – I'll be along in a minute."

Tom was as good as his word; the bootmaker and I had only just settled ourselves at the table in the back office when he came in with a tray. "The water had just boiled," he explained, before putting the tray down and leaving us alone.

"Now, Mr Humphries," I said, pouring him a cup and pushing it towards him. Tom was right about the bootmaker being shaken up; his hand trembled as he lifted the cup and he quickly steadied it with the other. He took a small sip and then replaced the cup carefully in the saucer.

"Constable Plank, I have come to you because I remember that you had a certain, well, delicacy in handling difficult matters. And today I have another difficult matter."

"A monetary concern?" I asked, reaching for my notebook.

He shook his head. "Not this time, no. It may be nothing – indeed, I pray it is nothing – but then again, it may be something dreadful."

I laid my pencil on my notebook and clasped my hands. "Mr Humphries," I said, using the gentle but firm tone I have tried so often to teach Wilson, "Mr Humphries, there is clearly something amiss. You have come to me, which is sensible, but I cannot help you while you talk in riddles."

The bootmaker swallowed hard and closed his eyes for a long moment. When he opened them again, he leaned towards me and said in a low tone, "It is Mr Welford – Josiah Welford. My leather cutter. He says that he has murdered his wife."

As Humphries and I walked down the steps of the police office I saw Wilson coming along the street towards us. Although the bootmaker had been adamant that his leather cutter was not a violent man, I took the view that someone who claimed to have murdered his wife should be treated with caution, and it seemed wise to have someone of Wilson's deterrent dimensions on hand. As we walked the short distance to Conduit Street I explained the bare bones of the matter to my junior constable; he raised an eyebrow but said nothing. I was glad to see that he is learning to keep his counsel, at least in front of others.

The bootmaker's premises were as I remembered them: a narrow shopfront consisting of the door and a window right alongside it, with the shop itself crowded with shelves to the ceiling, filled with boxes and lasts. As we pushed open the door a bell rang in the back of the shop – the workroom, I guessed.

"Is Mr Welford alone?" I asked Humphries.

He shook his head. "When I decided to come and see you, I thought it best not to leave him unattended – we have plenty of knives, scissors and the like, you see." He looked at me and I nodded. "Jem is in there too; he's a carpenter, a friend of mine, and he's pretending to measure for new cupboards. Big lad, just in case."

We walked through a door at the back of the shop into, as I had surmised, the workroom where the boots and shoes were made and repaired. The man I took to be Jem was standing in the middle of the room, a notebook in his hand, while another, much older, much slighter man was sitting at a bench. They both looked over at us.

Humphries indicated the man at the bench, who stood. "This is Mr Welford," he said. Welford was about sixty, I guessed, and almost as leathery as the man's boot he held in one hand while tidying its edges with the sole knife held in his other hand. His greying hair was neat, and his posture surprisingly good for a man who had spent, I imagined, four decades or more crouched over benches. He nodded his head in acknowledgement. "These are two constables, Josiah," continued Humphries, "come to talk to you about your wife. About what you told me about your wife."

I walked over towards Welford, lifting a stool that I passed and setting it alongside his bench. I sat and indicated that he should too. I tapped the bench with my hand, and he put down both the boot and the knife.

"Mr Welford," I said quietly, "Mr Humphries tells me that you have killed your wife."

The leather cutter looked up at me but I do not think he really saw me. He nodded but said nothing.

"Is that right, Mr Welford? Have you murdered your wife?"

He showed no reaction in his expression and simply nodded again.

"Did she anger you, Mr Welford? Did she shame you with her behaviour? Perhaps another man?" I asked.

This time there was something – a slight tear in the eye, I thought – but still no reply.

"Was she a bad wife, Mr Welford?" I asked.

He shook his head. "No, sir – she was a good wife to me, for nigh on forty years. A good wife. But," and he glanced over each shoulder in turn before leaning towards me and lowering his voice even further, "the message told me to do it."

"The message?" asked John Conant. Wilson and I had gone straight up to the magistrate's rooms as soon as we had returned to the police office. "A real message, or an imagined one? Is the man mad, do you think?"

I shook my head. "I think not, no, sir, as he seemed quite ordered in his thinking. Not mad, but rather simple, perhaps. Naive. Unquestioning. I asked him about the message and he talked of a gathering, and of his brethren."

The magistrate raised an eyebrow. "Brethren? Religious brethren?"

"The same thought occurred to me, sir," I said. "We asked Mr Humphries – the bootmaker – about it, and he said that for about a year now Mr Welford has been attending Methodist meetings."

Conant frowned slightly. "Methodist meetings? But the Methodists are a peaceable group, are they not? Hardly likely to encourage a man to do away with his wife."

I beckoned Wilson forward. "Constable Wilson had an idea about that, sir." I looked at Wilson and nodded. "Tell Mr Conant what you told me on the way here."

Wilson took a breath and began. "My mother, sir, Mrs Wilson. She has a friend, Mrs Farnell. Both widows, you see, sir. Not easy for them, sir, but my mother has me, bringing in my wages, while Mrs Farnell has only two daughters, both married now and living up north. They send her money, of course, but they live so far away. So she's on her own, really." Conant caught my eye; he was obviously wondering where this might lead.

"The Methodists, constable," I prompted.

Wilson nodded. "Mr Farnell was a Methodist, and Mrs Farnell joined when she married him, and now she has fallen in with a particular group of them – the ones who worship out of doors, in fields and the like."

"The Primitives, you mean?" asked the magistrate.

"Or the Ranters, as the news-sheets would have it," I said.

"My mother says that since Mrs Farnell started going to these outdoor services, she has been different. Trying to convert everyone, and talking of little but what the preacher has said." Wilson shook his head sadly. "And then when Mr Humphries said that Mr Welford had attended meetings in Cooper's Gardens, the name sounded familiar: that's where Mrs Farnell goes."

"Cooper's Gardens?" asked Conant. "Where is that?"

"Bethnal Green," I said. "About four miles from here."

"Four miles?" said the magistrate in surprise.

Wilson looked at me and I nodded. "Mrs Farnell says that there is nowhere nearer; it is difficult for them to find premises in which to worship. Many landlords do not trust them, and they do not have the money to build their own chapels."

Conant sighed. "And so they gather in fields."

"They also believe that it brings them closer to God, says Mrs Farnell," added Wilson. "Being outdoors, rather than under a roof."

"And it was at one of these meetings – these services – that someone told Mr Welford to kill his wife?" asked the magistrate.

"That is what we need to discover," I replied.

"Married for nearly forty years – she must have trusted him completely," said Martha sadly. "What would make a man do such a thing?"

I considered teasing her about keeping a man waiting for his dinner, but in all honesty I was in no mood for jest. As Martha sat down next to me I patted her hand.

"I think that Mr Welford is not quite right in the head. He kept saying that a message had told him to do it. Mr Conant wondered whether it was all in his imagination – whether he was hearing things."

Martha nodded as she blew lightly on her spoonful of broth. "I have heard of that, of people thinking that God is telling them what to do. And if God can speak to people, perhaps Old Harry can too."

"The Devil, you mean!" I shook my head. "Surely you cannot think that the Devil is going around whispering into men's ears, telling them to murder their wives! There is no such creature: what some call the Devil is simply the evil side of our own nature. We look for someone to blame for our own shortcomings."

Martha said nothing, but I could tell from the pink in her cheeks that my words had stung her. I shook my head again and we continued eating in silence. Any married man can tell you that there is a most uncomfortable quality to the particular silence that falls when your wife is displeased, and I felt it now.

"I'm sorry, Mar," I said. "I did not mean to make fun. Truly I did not." I reached under the table and squeezed her leg.

"Hmph," she said, using a piece of bread to mop around her bowl. "You are a clever man, Sam Plank, but there are plenty of things that you do not know. Only a fool thinks that he knows everything."

"Of course you are right, my love," I said. She looked across at me with narrowed eyes, checking for sarcasm, and I smiled contritely. She stood to clear the table, and I knew I was forgiven when she wordlessly handed me a slice of walnut loaf.

I always try to undress quickly and climb into bed so that I can enjoy watching my wife prepare for sleep. Although she is no longer a young woman she has kept the soft, neat shape that I find so desirable, and witnessing the delicate play of her hands over her hair as her fingertips search for pins and the gentle shiver with which she shrugs on her nightdress is for me a pleasure at the end of each day. But this evening, as she pulled up the covers and slipped into bed alongside me, craftily moving her chilly feet to warm them on my shins, I sighed more with sadness than with contentment.

Martha turned to me. "What is it, Sam? Are you hurting?" I shook my head. "Then what, Sam?" Still I said nothing. "You can tell me, Sam, or I can keep asking. And if you wish to sleep at all tonight, I suggest the first."

"I thought it did not matter, but it seems that it does," I said quietly. Martha moved her hand across my chest until it was resting over my heart – a calming, warming connection between us. "Mr Welford killed his wife in their bed. At night, like this. He put a pillow over her face while she slept, and she could not breathe. And lying here now, with you..." I stopped.

"Did you see her?" Martha asked.

"Yes," I said. "Mr Welford took us to her. She looked... calm. Peaceful. He had arranged her very carefully in the bed – respectfully, I thought."

"Well, that at least is something. And what has happened to him?"

"Welford? He was no trouble at all – meek as a lamb. He is spending the night in a cell at the police office, under the watchful eye of George Cooper. When I left, they were settling down to a game of draughts."

"Hah!" said Martha. "I hope Mr Welford does not put any money on the game – I've heard you say there's not a player in London to beat Mr Cooper." She turned her head to look up at me. "And tomorrow?"

"Tomorrow morning," I replied, "Mr Welford will appear before a magistrate. After that, it will be the house of correction, or – more likely – a madhouse."

Martha propped herself up on an elbow. "A madhouse? For killing his wife?"

I shook my head. "Not for the murder, no – that would be Newgate. At first, as I told Mr Conant, I didn't think Welford was mad – he seemed too calm, too sensible for that. No raving or shouting, no wild eyes or flailing limbs. But as we were leaving his bedroom, he called out a farewell to his wife, just as I do every morning to you. And then in the coach on the way to Great Marlborough Street he asked me to send word to his wife that he would be home late for supper. The poor man had quite forgotten that he had killed her."

CHAPTER TWO

A visit to Cooper's Gardens

SUNDAY 6TH JULY 1828

Martha tried hard to act as though she rode in a coach every day, but as we pressed on into High Holborn and the traffic both thickened and accelerated, her hand crept across the space between us on the seat and I took hold of it.

"At least we have fine weather for our excursion," I said lightly.

Martha gasped as a cart going the other way passed within a whisker of touching us, and I squeezed her hand.

"You should see it on a weekday," I said. "At least we are making good progress; I've often had to jump out and continue on foot, making better time than the horses."

"It was kind of Mr Conant to insist on paying for a coach for us," said Martha.

"If you are going to act as an unpaid constable for him," I said stoutly, "it is the least he can do – and four miles there and four miles back would be too much, with all the standing in between."

"Will there be a deal of standing?" asked Martha.

"Aye," I said, glancing out as we passed Newgate. As ever, the tall stone gateway was in the shadows – both morally and literally, as the keeper John Wontner often said. "It seems that people like to get their money's worth from the preachers: these meetings can last two hours or more."

The jarvey stopped on Hackney Road, saying that he could take his animals to the watermen's stand by Shoreditch Church, and I helped Martha to climb down from the coach. We turned into Crabtree Row – named, I guessed, in more rural times but now lined with modern brick houses – and walked to a small crossroads by the Birdcage public house. Here we left the road and struck off into the field that made up Cooper's Gardens; thankfully we had not had rain for several days and so the ground was hard and dry.

There was a crowd of about sixty people already waiting – young and old, slightly more women than men. At the centre of the gathering there was a wooden crate; I guessed that the preacher would stand on this to address the meeting. Martha and I kept to the edge of the group, as my intention was to watch rather than to participate. If Welford was to be believed, it was at a gathering such as this – mild though it seemed for the moment – that he was instructed to kill his wife. An earnest looking fellow, aged about thirty, neat and tidy, approached us and held out his hand, which I shook.

"George Robinson," he said. "Welcome – you are most welcome."

"Sam Plank," I said, "and my wife Martha."

Robinson nodded and smiled. "Perhaps you would like one of these to read later at your leisure."

He gave me a handbill, a few paragraphs printed on cheap paper, with the heading "The First Sermon and the Power of Peace".

"The subject of today's sermon by the Reverend Miller," he said, before nodding again and moving off to greet another new arrival.

The nearby church tolled the hour, and a man of about fifty years of age climbed up onto the crate – the Reverend Miller. He was dressed not as a minister of the church but in plain, sturdy clothes, such as a farmer might wear on market day, with only the white preaching bands to indicate his intent. He held in one hand a black book – no doubt his Bible – and the other hand he laid over his heart.

"Welcome, brothers and sisters," he said in warm tones that carried well – I guessed that this was not the first time he had addressed a crowd. "Welcome to you all, on this glorious day that our Lord has seen fit to send us. And on this glorious day we shall reflect on another, perhaps even more, glorious day: the day on which God sent down his first sermon."

The Reverend Miller was a good speaker: he moderated his voice to introduce excitement and despair, he used words that could be plainly understood yet which thrilled and engaged. By the time he reached the point in the story where Peter recounts what God has told him – the first sermon to the church – the whole crowd, whose numbers had now swelled to eighty or more, was listening in silence. He allowed his voice to quieten, requiring his audience – his congregation – to lean in to hear him. "The word which God sent was preaching peace by Jesus Christ. The first thing that God sends is peace. The proclamation this glorious day is, I am at peace with thee, be thou at peace with me. There is no thunder-bolt: God is a God of love to you. Every man here ought to believe that God is at peace with him, and believing it will make you at peace with him. His Son is the prince of peace – the Holy Ghost is the minister of peace – the first word in the commission given to the apostles is, peace be to this house. Peace be to this house." He looked downwards, eyes closed, hands clasping his Bible. "Peace be to every one of you. Amen."

"Amen," echoed the crowd, including Martha.

"And now my wife Sarah, who has heard the call from God to preach, would like to address the ladies. Gentlemen, if you would follow me, we shall continue our prayers and discussions."

I looked at Martha and raised my eyebrows.

"Off you go, Sam," she said, jerking her head towards the crowd of men that was moving off to another part of the field. "If you think I am going to miss the chance to hear a woman preacher, you're much mistaken."

After an hour of prayer and discussion quite unlike anything I had attended before – it seemed that anyone could raise his hand and address the group, talking of a revelation he had had or asking a question about how to interpret the Scriptures – we men were finally allowed to return to our womenfolk. By now my stomach was grumbling and I was keen to sample the slices of pie that I had seen Martha pack in her basket that morning. As I walked back towards her, I could see that Martha was engaged in close conversation with an old woman – seventy if she was a day. As my wife caught sight of me and smiled, her companion looked over her shoulder at me and then quickly took her leave of Martha, patting her on the arm in farewell and then – I thought, but surely not – touching Martha's belly before hurrying away.

"Who was that, my dear?" I asked.

"Mrs Wilkes," Martha replied, looking past me to the retreating back of the old woman. "You would have liked her, but she said she had to be on her way; a neighbour had offered her a ride home in his cart."

I offered Martha my arm and she took it, handing me her basket to carry. "I imagine that you are peckish, Sam, so I thought we could find a shady spot under a tree and have something to eat."

Quite how women manage to pack so much into a basket is beyond me – it must be a skill passed down the generations, for I remember my mother doing the same. First to come out was a blanket, which I spread on the grass before lowering myself onto it. Martha knelt beside me and unpacked our meal. Besides the pie, there was a crusty loaf, a paper bag of cherries – "Mind you eat those over the grass – I don't want to be scrubbing cherry juice out of that shirt when we get home" – a thick wedge of pound cake studded with currants, and a corked bottle of lemonade wrapped in a damp tea-towel to keep it cool. I pretended to take a swig from the bottle; Martha tutted and handed me two tumblers from the depths of the basket.

I took a bite of the pie and looked at Martha. "So," I said, "what did your woman preacher have to say?"

Martha gave a small shrug. "Much the same as a man preacher – nothing particularly, well, womanly."

"Womanly?" I repeated, smiling. "Still, it's unusual, isn't it – a woman leading a service. Even a service in a field."

"She's been doing it for ten years or more, apparently," Martha said, holding out her tumbler for more lemonade. "Her late father was a preacher, and she married a preacher, Mr Gregson, and when he died, she put it to them – the others at a meeting – that she should carry on his work. And they agreed; it turned out she had been writing his sermons all along. So now she travels the country with her second husband, preaching wherever she is needed."

"An itinerant preacher," I said.

"That's right," said Martha. "That's what she said – I didn't know the word." She looked at the food on the blanket. "More pie, or shall I wrap it up?"

"Another small piece, and then I'll move on to cake and cherries," I said. "And what about Mrs Wilkes? Is she a preacher too?"

"Oh no," said Martha, slicing the pie. "She just comes to listen, and for the company too, I think. She's local – lives in Whitechapel – so she knows most of those who come."

"You seemed to be deep in conversation with her," I said.

"Did I?" Martha took a sip of lemonade.

"And she did not want to meet me," I added. I paused. "Had you told her I am a constable?"

Martha sounded indignant. "I did tell her, yes, but I doubt she was avoiding you because of that. She was keen to be on her way with her friend and his cart, to save a long walk later."

"And did I see her put a hand on your belly?"

"My belly, Sam? What a peculiar suggestion!"

But a quarter-century as a married man and even longer as a constable has given me a good ear for a falsehood.

CHAPTER THREE

The queer plunger

MONDAY 7TH JULY 1828

The next morning, Martha asked me to accompany her to Oxford Market, which was on my way to Great Marlborough Street. We had just paused at the corner of the market to say farewell when I saw Wilson coming towards us at a great pace, his hand on his hat to keep it in place.

"Good morning, Mrs Plank. Good morning, sir," he said breathlessly. "I was coming to fetch you. Reports of a fight, sir. At the receiving house by the reservoir in Green Park. Another queer plunger."

"Another? That's the third this month," I said. "It's high time we put a stop to this shamming." Wilson was stepping from foot to foot, obviously keen to reach the brawl. "You go on ahead, lad, and I'll catch you up. No running unless you have to, remember."

My instruction fell on deaf ears as Wilson hared off down the street. At what age does a man stop running towards fights and choose instead to run from them, I wondered.

"What on earth is a queer plunger?" asked Martha.

"An irritation is what they are," I replied. Martha folded her arms and huffed slightly, and I remembered my manners. "After a number of drownings some fifty years ago," I explained, "two doctors set up what we now call the Royal Humane Society to encourage attempts to resuscitate the drowned. Receiving houses were established across London, equipped with life-saving equipment and instructions on what to do to revive someone. Anyone who does manage to save someone from drowning is given four guineas by the Society, as a reward."

Martha raised her eyebrows. "Four guineas! A fine sum."

"Indeed," I said, "and therein lies the problem. Rogues have worked out a way to bilk the system. They operate in pairs: one throws himself into the water and pretends to drown – he's the queer plunger – while the other pulls him out and carries him to the nearest receiving house. The rescuer is rewarded with his four guineas, and the revived fellow will pretend that he was driven to such extremes by great financial necessity, which he hopes will solicit further donations from soft-hearted bystanders."

"Quite a scheme," observed Martha. "But dangerous too – what if he really does drown?"

I shrugged. "No doubt that does happen. And often people will realise that they have been duped, and will take matters into their own hands – as I suspect has happened today at the reservoir." I leaned across and kissed Martha on the cheek. "And so I must go and pour oil on troubled waters."

By the time I arrived at Green Park, perhaps fifteen minutes later, the situation had calmed down. Wilson was standing outside the receiving house – not one built for the purpose, like the grand one near the Serpentine, but simply one of the park keepers' buildings – with another man, who had a pile of dark cloth at his feet. A small crowd of curious onlookers waited nearby, and from time to time there was a banging from the receiving house, as though someone was knocking loudly on the door from the inside.

Wilson stepped forward to meet me.

"Constable Plank," he said, "this is Mr Ward, Under Park Keeper." Mr Ward and I shook hands. "And that noise you can hear", continued Wilson, as we all turned in response to a fresh bout of banging, "is the much-recovered victim."

"A miraculous return to health," I said.

"Mr Ward is a volunteer with the..." Wilson looked at the park keeper.

"The Royal Humane Society," said that gentleman. "I have been instructed in the techniques of resuscitation. Using the bellows. And that man," he pointed angrily at the receiving house, "that man is no more drowned than I am. He is a cheat, sir – a thief and a disgrace."

Someone in the small crowd said, "Hear, hear!"

"And what has become of the man who rescued him from the water?" I asked.

"Gone," said Mr Ward. "Took to his heels."

"There is a bell," explained Wilson, pointing. "When someone is pulled from the water and taken to the receiving house, a placard outside explains that they are to ring the bell to summon a volunteer..."

"And I come running," interrupted the park keeper. "I am the volunteer. I have received instruction in these matters."

"Indeed," I said. "And what happened when you came running this morning?"

A few of the people from the little crowd moved slightly closer. Ward, sensing an audience, warmed to his theme. "As I say, I have received instruction in how to deal with such an emergency. I heard the bell; I was working further down the Queen's Walk, but I left my duties immediately and came running. Outside the receiving house I found two men: one was lying on the floor, and the other was leaning over him. Both were wet. I assumed that the one had pulled the other from the reservoir."

"A fair assumption," said one of the onlookers.

Ward nodded. "I told the rescuer – for that was what I assumed him to be – to help me drag the dead man – for such he seemed – into the receiving house. We lifted him onto the table and started to take off his wet outer garments and wrap him in dry blankets. This is the first step of resuscitation. I have received instruction, you know."

I caught Wilson's eye and he quickly looked away.

"And then what happened?" I asked.

"I took the bellows from the cupboard and told the rescuer to put them into the corpse's mouth. As he did so, the scarf that the rescuer had pulled up across his own face fell away, and I recognised him." Ward paused; the onlookers crept even closer. They looked at me expectantly, and I realised my role.

"Who was he, sir?" I asked.

"He was the very corpse I had helped to revive only the week before!" said the park keeper triumphantly. Someone in the crowd gasped. "I knew this was not a coincidence. The two men were in collusion, sir, to cheat me, and to cheat money from the Royal Humane Society!" He shook his head. "Once he saw that I knew him, he fled. His companion – by now fully alive again – would have followed, but he was wearing only his undergarments and no boots, and I ran out past him, grabbed his clothes and locked him in." Ward pointed to the dark pile at his feet. "And then I sent a lad for the constables."

"I see," I said. "Constable Wilson, I am going to talk to the gentleman in the building. Would you bring his clothes and then stand guard to waylay him should he try to escape. The key if you please, Mr Ward, and perhaps you could stand over there with the others." I held out my hand and nodded towards the small group of observers. The park keeper was about to object and I said quickly, "He may well be armed." This did the trick, and Ward moved swiftly away to safety.

Wilson and I walked towards the receiving house. The banging continued. Wilson dropped the dripping clothes in a heap and then surveyed his surroundings. He took hold of a bench overlooking the reservoir and dragged it so that it all but blocked the door of the building. When he was happy with the position of both the bench and himself, he nodded to me.

I knocked on the door. "Hello in there," I said. "I am Constable Plank of the Great Marlborough Street police office. With me I have a very large and determined constable, a smaller but angry park keeper, and a good number of interested bystanders. I also have your clothes. I am about to unlock the door and come in, and I expect you to be sensible. Is that clear?"

I waited for a moment, and then heard, "Yes."

"Stand away from the door," I said.

I looked at Wilson, who nodded, and then I unlocked the door. I opened it and looked into the receiving house. Against the far wall was a slight man, dressed – as Ward had said – in his undergarments, with boots on his feet and a blanket pulled about him. Using one hand to secure the blanket, he raised the other in surrender. I could tell at once that he had no intention of bolting. I indicated that Wilson should hand me the man's sodden clothing and I carried it at arm's-length into the building, putting it onto the table. Wilson closed the door behind me.

"You'll want to wring those out before putting them back on," I said, nodding at the clothes, which had started dripping onto the floor. "Although perhaps..." I walked to a cupboard and opened the doors. "Ah: as I thought. Spare dry clothes. Here." I took out a shirt and a coat. "You'll have to wear your own trousers, but at least you'll be only half damp."

I busied myself reading the large sheet of directions pinned up on the wall – Mr Ward's instructions – while the man dressed. When I looked over at him, he was running his fingers through his hair, trying to smooth it down.

"Well now, your name if you would," I said, taking out my notebook.

The man hesitated but eventually said, "Keane. Tobias Keane."

"And the name of your rescuer?" I asked. He shook his head and said nothing. "No matter," I continued. "And your purpose in undertaking this mischief?"

He cleared his throat. "The reward. The money for saving someone from drowning. We was going to split it – a guinea each."

I raised an eyebrow and smiled. "But the reward is four guineas. I think your friend was short-changing you, Mr Keane."

"More than likely," he said, before a cough overtook him. He felt in the pocket of the borrowed coat with one hand, keeping the other hand over his mouth, and eventually I handed him my handkerchief, which he took with a nod and pressed to his lips. Once the coughing fit had passed, he looked over at me. "Will you arrest me, sir?"

I closed my notebook. "Mr Ward has been greatly inconvenienced by you this morning. I think it only right that he – and our little audience out there – see me take you off to Great Marlborough Street."

Keane sighed and walked towards me. I knocked on the door and Wilson opened it. I indicated that Keane should walk between us, and we passed the park keeper and his chorus as we made for Piccadilly. Mr Ward nodded with satisfaction and returned to the receiving house, presumably to tidy it in readiness for its next use.

We turned eastwards on Piccadilly and then left into Berkeley Street. In the shadow of Devonshire House I stopped. Wilson and Keane walked on for a couple of steps before realising and then returned to me.

"I think we shall part company here, Mr Keane," I said.

Keane started in surprise and looked from me to Wilson and back again, as if suspecting a trick. I nodded, and he turned and walked away towards Berkeley Square, once looking back over his shoulder and then putting his head down and disappearing into an alleyway.

Wilson and I continued up Berkeley Street and turned into Bruton Street. He said nothing.

"Aren't you going to ask why I did that?" I said after a few minutes.

Wilson shook his head. "I assume you have a good reason, sir," he said.

"It is all a matter of balance," I explained as we crossed into Conduit Street and passed Limmer's Hotel. "The real villain of the piece is long gone. The Royal Humane Society has not lost any money, and that crowd in Green Park has seen that anyone who tries to cheat the system will be taken away by the constables. Keane has had a good soaking and a serious fright, and now he feels beholden to us." I paused as we waited to cross Regent Street. "On balance, you see, we have done well: no papers to process, and a rogue in our pocket who is already reflecting on the company he keeps."

Back at the police office, I climbed the stairs to Mr Conant's rooms to tell him what I had discovered the previous day at Cooper's Gardens. I found him putting on his coat and gathering the papers from his table in order to attend his hearings at ten o'clock. I knew how he detested tardiness, so I accompanied him down the stairs and through into the chamber behind the courtroom where magistrates assembled before taking the bench.

"Mrs Plank and I went to Cooper's Gardens," I explained as we walked, "and stayed for the entire gathering. There was a sermon for everyone, and then we separated into two groups for prayer and discussion – one led by the preacher and the other by his wife."

"His wife?" repeated Conant as he signalled to the court clerk that he was ready to start the morning's business.

"Quite usual, I am told," I replied, "among these particular Methodists. And neither Mrs Plank nor I saw anything of any messages or instructions, beyond the usual reminders to pray regularly and be good to your fellow man."

"As we feared, then, with Mr Welford," said the magistrate, looking at me. "Quite mad. I shall make sure to add this to his notes before they are sent to the judge."

CHAPTER FOUR

Martha and Mrs Miller

SATURDAY 12TH JULY 1828

The following Saturday evening I was damping down the stove when Martha carried in the clothes horse to air some linens in front of it overnight. As she laid them over the rails, making sure that they were straight and not wrinkled, she asked me what I had in mind for the next day.

"Tomorrow?" I said, leaning the poker against the wall and, taking care that Martha should not see me, wiping my hands on the back of my trousers.

"I was thinking that I would go to the service at Cooper's Gardens," she said. "Mrs Miller is speaking again."

"And how do you know that?" I asked. "I thought she moved on each week, speaking wherever she was needed."

Martha straightened up and put her hands on her hips, which is rarely a good sign. "You can take that tone out of your voice right now, Samuel Plank," she said sharply. "I am not one of your arrests, being questioned in that back office at Great Marlborough Street, thank you very much. I know because Mrs Wilkes has sent word."

"Mrs Wilkes? The old woman you were talking to?" I asked. Martha nodded. "But I was hoping to mend that kitchen drawer tomorrow. The one that sticks."

"And you still can," said Martha quickly. "I was not suggesting that you come as well. Mrs Wilkes has a grandson who lives near here, and he has agreed to take me in his cart. He'll be calling for me at eight, so you can meet him. He's a coal man."

"Well, I hope he gives his cart – and himself – a good wash beforehand," I said lightly. "It won't do to hear God's word in a smutty frock." But Martha did not smile.

CHAPTER FIVE

A reader of men

MONDAY 14TH JULY 1828

As was now our habit, Wilson knocked lightly on the back door just as I was finishing my breakfast. It had been an all but silent meal; Martha had laid the food on the table with good enough grace, but she resisted all my attempts to draw her into conversation, just as she had done the previous evening. In particular, she seemed reluctant to talk about her visit to Cooper's Gardens, from where she had returned in the middle of the afternoon.

"You were right about that coal dust" was her only comment, before she asked me to put out the tub for her Sunday evening bath. I offered to scrub her back but she was in no mood for teasing and shooed me away into the kitchen. She had fallen asleep quickly, and in the morning went about her tasks without her normal chatter. I missed it more than I would have imagined. Even Wilson noticed it, and young men are not known for their sensitivity to these matters.

"I don't mean to stick my nose in," he said as we walked south towards Oxford Street, "but is Mrs Plank unwell? She seemed very quiet." I glanced at him and saw concern on his open face.

"As a bachelor," I replied, "you will be unaware of the changeability of the female mood."

Wilson barked a laugh. "Unaware! You should try living in close quarters with my sister Sal – there's changeability for you."

We stopped to allow a cart loaded with flowers to continue its journey eastwards and an empty hackney, looking for custom, to amble past westwards, and then crossed Mortimer Street. I did not want to admit my unease to Wilson, as this would only increase his own, so I simply smiled in acknowledgement and turned our talk to professional matters.

Wilson and I walked into the front office at Great Marlborough Street, where Tom Neale was frowning as he looked at the sheets of paper spread across his counter. Tom was an office keeper beyond compare – I knew this from hearing constables from other police offices complaining about the individuals with whom they had to deal – and almost the only thing that would ruffle his feathers was a stack of papers. Tom liked people, not paper, as he was fond of saying.

He looked up at us and shook his head. "Barely half past eight," he said sorrowfully, "and already six warrants ready to go. That's what comes of not observing the correct order and hours of business."

"Late hearings again?" I asked.

"Late luncheon, more like," said Tom. "If only they were all like Mr Conant, and as diligent."

"Indeed," I said. In the same way as I knew from others how fortunate we were with our office keeper, I was also aware that Mr Conant's dedication to his work – his determination to read all his papers, and his insistence on sitting at his hearings for the correct hours and not allowing his stomach to distract his brain – was unusual among magistrates and much to be prized.

"Now, Sam, as you and young William are the first in, you have your pick of these," said Tom, indicating the warrants on the counter. "I can offer a toper, a pair of cracksmen (brothers, by the look of it), a shoplifter, her fence, and a nose."

"The nose," I said, an idea occurring to me. "Where is he?"

Tom glanced at the warrant and then handed it to me. "Right up your street, Sam – or it would be, if you lived on Newgate Street."

I felt Wilson looking over my shoulder at the other warrants. "Do you fancy a leg-stretch to Newgate?" I asked.

"Not a chance," he said, as I had known he would. By the time we reached the office every morning he was itching to get to work; the prospect of a long walk before any action would not please him. "I'll wait a few minutes for John," he named another of the younger constables, "and see if he fancies tackling the brothers with me."

By the time I turned into Newgate Street, I was wondering whether Wilson had made the wiser choice after all. The sun had disappeared behind a thick cloak of purpling clouds before I had reached Aldwych, and rain started coming down in the fat drops of a summer storm. When I could I walked in the lee of buildings but they offered little protection and I was soon soaked. I banged on the heavy wooden door of the gaol, calling my name in answer to the enquiry from within, and the turnkey hauled it open to admit me. I did not recognise him, but he of course read my uniform.

"Take a tumble in the river on the way here, did you, constable?" he asked, making a noise at the back of his throat that I assumed was a sound of appreciation at his own sharp wit. "Mind now, there's no need for that." This as I took off my hat and shook my shoulders like a dog.

"Is the keeper in his office?" I asked, brushing more water from the brim of my hat.

"When I am gifted with seeing through walls, sir, I shall be able to tell you," replied the turnkey, with another gurgle. "In the meantime, perhaps you would care to head that way yourself and have a look."

"Ah yes, that will be Gordy Martin," said John Wontner, taking my coat from me, shaking it outside his office door, and then hanging it to drip on a nail on the wall. "Just come to us from Millbank – he has not the lungs for the marshes of Pimlico, as you probably heard."

"Aye," I said, pointing to my own throat. "Here." Wontner nodded. "But he is, well…"

"A dry boots?" suggested the keeper. It was my turn to nod. "His jests may not be to everyone's taste," he continued, "but I take the view that humour in a prison is no bad thing. We'll see if he's still joking in a few months' time."

Once again, I was reminded of why John Wontner was that rarest of men: a prison keeper trusted by the authorities, admired by those who worked with him, and obeyed by those under his care. He had never been one to insist on rules for their own sake, but enforced them only when they served their purpose. So a jesting turnkey might not be welcome at many gaols, but at Newgate laughter was a commodity to be treasured.

"The usual? Or tea, to warm your old bones?" asked Wontner. Our usual refreshment was the seemingly bottomless pitcher of barley water that he kept on his desk, but he was right: after my soaking I needed something hot. He called down the corridor for a tray of tea and we talked of this and that while we waited, and then while he poured. When we were both settled, he looked at me and raised an eyebrow.

"Ah yes, of course," I said, and reached over to dig into the deep side pocket of my still-dripping coat for the warrant. "I need to talk to one of your recent arrivals – Jack Lynch."

Wontner put down his cup and turned to the ever-present stack of papers on his desk. There must have been some method to it, for it took him only moments to find the relevant document. "Housebreaking," he said, glancing down the sheet. "Claims that he was only the lookout, and that he was coerced."

"That makes sense," I said. "Apparently he wants to turn King's evidence."

Wontner sighed. "A dangerous business. If I were a young bachelor," he glanced at the paper to check the details, "yes, in his shoes I'm not sure I wouldn't take my chances with transportation to Australia, rather than spend the rest of my life looking over my shoulder here in London." We both sat in silence for a minute or two, Wontner wordlessly refilling our cups. "And now, Sam," he said eventually, "perhaps you feel revived enough to tell me what's really on your mind."

"So you fancy yourself a reader of men, do you?" I said. It came out more sharply than I had intended; perhaps my mood was more sour than I had realised.

"I do, yes, Sam," Wontner replied mildly. "And we both know that you have come here to talk of something other than the treachery of Mr Lynch. Out with it, my fine fellow." He smiled encouragingly. "From your reluctance and slight flush, I suspect the involvement of a lady, so either your eye has wandered from Mrs Plank..."

"Never!" I said hotly. "I could never betray..." I stopped. "Hah. Well-played, John."

The keeper inclined his head in a mocking bow. "Thank you. And now that you have broached the subject successfully, you can tell me what is really troubling you about Mrs Plank."

I took a breath and straightened my shoulders. "As you know, Martha and I have no children. What you do not know is that," I closed my eyes momentarily, "is that Martha has been with child. Three times. And not a single baby to show for it."

"I am grieved to hear of your losses, Sam," said Wontner. "Truly I am. My wife and I, we too have felt a child quicken, only to lose it."

"But you – you have been rewarded with other children," I said, looking across at him.

"Rewarded? That is the word you choose. You think that we are more deserving of children than you and your wife?" he asked.

I shrugged. "In all honesty, John, I am at a loss to find an explanation. We are good people, Martha and I – she by far the better of the pair, of course." I tried a weak smile. "We are both hale. Martha still prays for a little addition to our home." The keeper looked at me questioningly. "I am not convinced that prayers are often answered and so I leave that to her," I explained. "And despite our sadness we had, after so long, made our peace with what we do have. We are very fond of each other, as you know, and I do not undervalue that. We have Alice and little Martha, and Wilson, and Martha's girls at the school – we are not starved of young company. And perhaps our chance to be parents has finally gone. Martha is not a young woman any longer." I sighed. "And I am not a young man."

"And so what has changed?" asked Wontner. "You said that you *had* made your peace – but it seems that this peace has vanished. What has disturbed it?"

"You were right," I said. "You are indeed a reader of men." I leaned forward in my seat, elbows on my knees and my hands clasped – almost praying, I realised. "It is Martha. I think she is starting to hope again. Or rather, someone is encouraging her to hope again. She has been attending Methodist prayer meetings, with a woman preacher, and when she comes home, she is distracted. Quiet. Turned in on herself." I looked up at the keeper. "Even Wilson has noticed."

"And have you asked her what is distressing her?"

"I have tried, but I am clumsy. I can question any number of rogues and cheats – even murderers – but my own wife... There I cannot find the right words to induce her to tell me." I stopped.

"Of course you cannot," said Wontner stoutly. "You do not care for the rogues and cheats and murderers, and you will not have to face them over the supper table when your questioning is complete. There is much at stake when examining a loved one." He drew a piece of paper towards him and picked up a pencil. "I have an idea about how we could proceed, but first tell me what you noticed about Mrs Plank's behaviour that seems to you to be out of the ordinary. And," he looked over at me, "in particular, why you think it has anything to do with babies."

CHAPTER SIX

Grace by name

SATURDAY 19TH JULY 1828

For about the tenth time that morning Martha made some excuse or other to return to our bedroom, and I knew that if I followed her I would catch her peering into the looking glass. My wife is not a vain woman – far from it, although to my mind she has cause to be, as I find her beautiful – but the imminent arrival of John Wontner and his wife had made her determined to look her very best.

As the keeper had suggested, I had invited them to visit us, saying to Martha that I knew John so well that it was high time for them to meet. Martha had quizzed me relentlessly when I arrived home with the news. Was Mrs Wontner an educated woman? How old was she? Did she have children?

I gave as much information as I had. Grace Wontner was the daughter of a clergyman, taught to read and write alongside her brothers. She was thirty-seven years old, and had three children. I already knew, from seeing her work on the wall of her husband's office, that as a younger woman – before life as a wife and mother had demanded more of her time – she had enjoyed painting pictures of her family and had shown some skill at it.

At precisely noon there was a knock on the front door, and I opened it, Martha standing behind me putting a final assessing hand to her hair. She need not have worried: as soon as Grace Wontner walked in, her warmth put us all at ease and it was immediately obvious that the two women would become firm friends.

"Mrs Plank," she said, holding out both her hands to take hold of Martha's, "I cannot tell you how excited I have been at the thought of meeting you. John is always talking about your husband and I have grown rather envious. Why should they be the only ones to enjoy conversations and consultations? And here you are, exactly as I pictured you. My name is Grace."

Martha smiled, and tucked one of Grace's hands into the crook of her arm to lead her into the sitting room. "And mine is Martha," she said. "Come: you must be in need of refreshment after that journey – the roads are so dusty. The gentlemen can join us if they wish, although perhaps Mr Wontner would prefer the George and

Dragon." My wife did not often encourage me to visit a public house, so I needed no second bidding: in one neat movement Wontner replaced his hat on his head and turned on his heel, and he and I left the ladies to their tea.

Once we were settled in a quiet corner of the George and Dragon, a tankard in front of each of us, we smiled at each other.

"The best laid plans..." said Wontner, shaking his head.

"Indeed," I agreed. "I had all manner of schemes in mind to find an excuse to leave them alone together, and within a minute of meeting they threw us out." I took a long draught of my beer. "I hope Mrs Wontner can find out what I could not."

Wontner looked at me levelly. "Grace was brought up in a vicarage, listening to the concerns of her father's parishioners. She then – Heaven only knows why – agreed to marry a city marshal, and stood by me when I was invalided out of that. And now she puts up with Newgate. She hears it all, Sam, as I know your wife does too. Without them we would be sorry fellows indeed." He raised his tankard in salute and I did likewise. "I think they will quickly find that they have much in common, and the confidences will flow."

"Grace Wontner seems a nice person," I said conversationally as I sat in bed that night waiting for Martha to join me. She had her back to me as she pulled the pins from her hair, and I enjoyed watching the neat movements of her fingers. "Of course I knew she would be: John Wontner would not have chosen otherwise." The last of Martha's curls sprang loose and she shook her head. I held up the covers; she slid into bed and tucked herself into my side, her head on my chest. "Did you talk about anything in particular?" I asked.

"We did, as it happens," said Martha. "We talked about what clever men we had married." I sensed a trap and said nothing. "Grace told me that you and Mr Wontner had cooked up a scheme to find out what was worrying me, and that you had recruited her to your cause."

"It was not a scheme," I protested. "I merely mentioned to John that you seemed preoccupied, and he suggested that you might be more, well, that you might find it easier to talk to another woman, and..." I stopped talking because Martha had put her finger across my lips.

She looked up at me. "I am sorry that you felt you had to go to such lengths. I know that I have been quiet lately. But I did not want to distress you."

I caught hold of her hand and kissed it. "Nothing distresses me as much as the thought that you cannot talk to me, my love," I said. I took a deep breath. "Is it our childlessness that preoccupies you?" I asked. She nodded. "And why now, my dear? It has been this way for so long."

Martha was quiet for several minutes. It took all of my strength not to say anything more, but if I filled the silence then she would not. She moved away from me so that we could see each other, our faces inches apart on our pillows. Her brown eyes were dark and serious.

"Three months ago, Sam," she said quietly, "I thought there was a baby. And for two months there was a baby." She blinked. "And then there was not."

"But you said nothing to me," I said.

"We have travelled this road many times before, Sam. And it has made me selfish." I opened my mouth to reply, but Martha continued. "Selfish, Sam, because I find it easier to bear my own disappointment than yours."

I looked into her eyes. "Have there been many more, my dear? Since the three?" I asked.

"A few," she said quietly. "Four. Perhaps five – although I was less certain that time."

"Five times you have had this sadness alone. Five times. And I did not see it," I said.

"That is not true, Sam. This time you did see."

"The old woman at the Methodist meeting – she touched your belly," I said, remembering. "Was that when you were still..."

Martha nodded. "Mrs Wilkes. She said she had a sense for these things, that she could tell when a woman was with child." She smiled. "All nonsense, of course: she had seen me looking a bit green, and chucking someone else's baby under the chin, and touching my own belly – all the signs were there for anyone who was looking. And old women have plenty of time for looking."

"So why was she so shifty when she saw me?"

"Something and nothing, Sam." Martha reached up to tuck a loose curl behind her ear. "When I said that yes, I thought I was expecting, she said she knew all manner of herbs and remedies to help me along if I wanted a boy, or a whip-smart baby. Nothing dangerous I don't think," she said hurriedly as she saw the look in my eye, "and I told her that I wasn't interested, that I would be happy with whatever baby God saw fit to send me. I said that my husband was a constable and had seen plenty of women suffering the after-effects of all sorts of remedies." She smiled. "She's an old woman, Sam – living in the past, remembering how it was when she had her little ones." The smile faded. "And when I saw her the following week, and told her that... well, when I told her, she was very kind."

I reached across and, with the back of my fingers, stroked Martha's cheek. "I am pleased, my dearest wife, that someone was there with kindness when you needed it. But I am sorrier than I can say that it was not your husband. Please, Martha, please: promise me that you will not keep such things from me again. It will break my heart, yes, as it breaks yours – but we promised 'in sickness and in health'. In heart-break and in joy."

Martha nodded silently.

CHAPTER SEVEN

Sickness at the Blue Boar

TUESDAY 29TH JULY 1828

Martha's promise to keep nothing from me was tested sooner than either of us would have wished. It was barely a fortnight later when I came home in the evening to find her sitting at the table in the kitchen, still wearing her bonnet, and our dinner still in the basket at her feet. She looked up as I came in, and her eyes were dark and frightened in her pale face. I quickly sat down next to her and took her hand, which was cold and trembling.

"What is it, my dear?" I asked.

"Little Martha," she said. "And two of the Atkins children. All sick."

"Sick?" I said. "Sick with what?"

"At first Alice thought it was just a cold," said Martha. "You know how little ones are, with their sniffles and snuffles." She smiled weakly. "But two days ago, Alice says, the coughing started." She squeezed my hand. "Oh Sam, it's awful to hear. The poor little mites struggling for breath, and then a great sucking in of air, and then that coughing – with a whoop in it, just as they say." A tear fell from the corner of Martha's eye. "Chincough, Sam. We're almost certain."

My heart sank. No constable who has ever had cause to look through the burial records of any church could fail to realise the likely outcome; whooping cough, with its exhausting fits of coughing, quickly takes its toll on the youngest and the oldest. But still, treatments were improving all the time, and perhaps it was not even what we feared.

"Has Alice consulted an apothecary, or a physician?" I asked.

"The apothecary has advised keeping little Martha warm in bed, and dosing her with tartar emetic to make her vomit," said Martha. "Alice tries to do as she is told, but, oh Sam, I think it is just making little Martha weaker. Her poor little face today – and when I held her hand, it was so limp."

"Tartar emetic!" I snorted. "It seems to be their answer to everything. Next they'll be telling Alice to stick bits of brown paper on the child's head."

I stood and reached for my coat.

"Where are you going, Sam?" asked Martha. "Not to the Blue Boar to see little Martha – not at this time of night."

I shook my head. "No, not there. I'm going to see Mr Conant and ask if he would be willing to send his physician to look at the children."

All was dark downstairs at Great Marlborough Street but – as I had expected – a light was still visible in the magistrate's dining room upstairs. John Conant had his own house, of course – a fine terraced mansion in Portland Place – but he frequently stayed in the rooms above the courthouse. I knocked on the door and heard the magistrate's footman Williams hurrying down the stairs.

"Billy," I said as he opened the door, and I removed my hat so that he could see me more clearly in the light cast by the hallway lantern.

"Constable Plank," he replied in acknowledgement.

"Is he…?" I asked, casting my eyes upward.

"He is indeed," said Williams, standing aside to let me enter. "Miss Lily is staying with friends on the Isle of Wight." It was common knowledge that the widowed magistrate relied on the energetic and fond company of his daughter, and found Portland Place dreary in her absence. I followed Williams up the stairs and he announced me at the door to the dining room before withdrawing to attend to some footman's duty or other.

Mr Conant was sitting by the fire, spectacles on his nose, papers on his lap, and a glass of dark liquid on the low table to his side.

"Sam," he said warmly, looking up. "Thank goodness you are here, as these latest pronouncements concerning pay and expenses are – as you see – driving me to drink. And not just any drink: rum." He lifted the glass and took a sip. "Lily will not allow it in the house; she says it is no drink for a gentleman. But when that gentleman has spent years at sea, Sam, he develops a taste for it. May I offer you a tot?"

I shook my head. "I was once fond of it, sir," I said, "but if there is one thing guaranteed to make me cropsick, it is rum."

"And a cropsick constable we do not want," said the magistrate, indicating the other chair drawn close to the fire. "Come. Sit and tell me what tempts you from the side of the lovely Mrs Plank this evening." This comment, and the slight flush in Conant's cheeks, suggested that this was not his first glass of rum.

"The lovely Mrs Plank is rather distressed this evening," I said as I sat. "You will remember Alice Godfrey, the young mother we took in, who is now living at the Blue Boar in Holborn."

Conant nodded. "She named her child after your wife, did she not? A touching gesture, I always thought."

"Indeed," I said. "And Martha – Mrs Plank – has remained close to Alice and her daughter." I leaned forward. "This evening she returned from visiting them, and she says that the little girl is sick. They are of the view that it is chincough."

"Whooping cough?" asked Conant. I nodded. "Then I am very sorry to hear it. The child is – what – two years old?"

"Barely that," I said.

"And the diagnosis is certain?"

"Alice has very little money," I said. "Her room and board is provided by the landlord of the Blue Boar, where she helps with his children. Two of them are sick as well – the other four have been sent to stay with relatives until the danger has passed. But Alice is a simple girl, without means, and she relies on the apothecary and old wives' tales."

"And they are telling her to bleed the child, or roast her in an airless room, or make her vomit again and again?" asked the magistrate, bitterness in his voice.

"I believe so, yes," I said. "And this is why I have come to you. I would not ask for myself, you know that. But you are the father of a beloved daughter and know better than I the anguish young Alice is feeling. If it were Miss Lily, what would you do?"

Conant was already on his feet and walking to his desk. He took a piece of paper from the drawer and scribbled a note on it. "The Blue Boar in Holborn, you said?" he asked. I nodded. He wrote a few more words, then folded the paper, addressed it and handed it to me.

"Give this to Thin Billy on your way out. I do not mind whether it goes this evening or tomorrow morning, as long as it is there before breakfast. You might like to call on Miss Godfrey yourself first thing; she could well be unnerved dealing with Doctor Lockhart alone."

As I went into the hallway and knocked gently on the door leading to the servants' quarters, I glanced at the note. It was addressed to Doctor Lockhart of 22 Red Lion Square, which was only a matter of yards from the Blue Boar.

CHAPTER EIGHT

The wisdom of Doctor Lockhart

WEDNESDAY 30TH JULY 1828

The next morning Martha was quiet and determined as she completed her chores. I had sent word to Thomas Neale the previous evening – by way of the same message lad that Thin Billy had whistled up for the doctor – that I would not be walking to Great Marlborough Street first thing. And so I was rather surprised, at just gone seven o'clock, to hear Wilson's usual light knock on the back door.

"Did you not receive a message from Mr Neale?" I asked as I opened the door. "I sent him word that I had other matters to attend to first thing."

"I did, sir, yes," said Wilson, twisting his hands as he stood in the yard. "But I wanted to explain to you that I also have matters to attend to this morning. Personal matters of a private nature." He straightened a little as he delivered this impressive phrase, but he still looked miserable.

I raised an eyebrow. Martha walked up behind me. "Good morning, William," she said. "I'm afraid I can't cook you anything this morning, but there's some bread on the table, under a cloth, and some marmalade, if Sam has left you any. Now, Sam, we must be off, or Alice will wonder just who this physician is when he turns up." She reached for her hat.

"Physician?" asked Wilson. "A physician for Alice?"

Martha pushed past me and laid a hand on Wilson's arm. "Not for Alice, no, William. But for little Martha and two of the Atkins children. Mr Conant has arranged for his physician to call this morning, and if he arrives before we do…" She turned to look at me. "Coat, Sam."

Wilson looked confused. "But it was Alice I was going to see."

"Your personal matters of a private nature," I said as I pulled the door closed behind us.

Wilson reddened slightly and nodded. "She sent word to me yesterday that she wanted to see me. She said that Mrs Plank had been to see her and that she didn't want to worry her again."

"Worry me? Worry me?" said Martha as she led us down the street at a smart pace. "It is not a case of worrying, it is a case of caring. Well, she will have quite the party turning up on her doorstep today. And Sam, as we're three now, perhaps we could see our way to a coach rather than shanks' pony."

We could see that the yard of the Blue Boar was at its busiest when our coach stopped at the corner of Dean Street and Eagle Street. Eight o'clock was an important hour in the coaching timetable: passengers would have had their breakfast, and with long distances to cover before a midday break, the coachmen were keen on a prompt departure. Wilson and I stood either side of Martha, protecting her from the jostling as porters, ostlers, coachmen and passengers – all with an eye on the large clock in the yard – rushed through their last-minute preparations. Coach after coach – eight in all – rumbled past us heading for High Holborn, and as the last left the yard, I caught sight of George Atkins, the innkeeper, standing at the door with his arm above his head in extravagant farewell. He saw the three of us waiting on the threshold and waved us over.

"Welcome, welcome," he said. "Is it not a magnificent sight? I see it six mornings a week, and it never fails to stir me. What a country we live in – what a city!" His face fell. "But I forget myself. In truth, I try to forget."

He stood aside and ushered us into the hallway and down the corridor to the parlour. Once Martha had taken a seat – Wilson, like me, preferred to remain standing – Atkins all but collapsed into the chair next to hers. Martha leaned across and put a hand on his arm.

"How are they, George?" she asked.

"Maria and Alice have been up all night," he replied. "They made me go to bed at midnight, as I have to be up at five, but I doubt they had more than an hour's rest between them. I went upstairs at about six to see the little ones, and Thomas seems much better. He was breathing more easily, and Maria said that he had slept quietly."

"Thank Heavens," said Martha. "And what of Jane, and little Martha?"

The innkeeper laid his hand over Martha's. "No change with either of them. It is the coughing – it wears them out. They are so tiny, both of them. Nothing we do seems to help them." His head dropped. "Our poor little girls."

Martha took a breath. She had faced plenty of sickness and tragedy in her life, and found comfort – as do I – in practicality. "George, there may be something we can do. Sam's magistrate – Mr Conant – has arranged for his physician to call here this morning and give his advice."

Atkins looked up at me. "A physician?" he asked. "But how will we pay?"

I shook my head. "There is no thought of payment. Mr Conant is a father himself, and he sends you, with his compliments, what he hopes will be of most use."

Just then the potboy – a lanky lad of about fifteen with a sturdy canvas apron tied around him – appeared at the door. "If you please, Mr Atkins, there's a gentleman to see you. Says he's a vision." And into the room stepped Leonard Lockhart.

"A physician, I fear, rather than a vision," said the doctor. Younger than I had expected, Doctor Lockhart was a tall man, with a build more suited to manual labour than to the gentleness of the sick room. But his face fitted his profession: there was a concerned intelligence to his eyes. He was dressed in sombre, well-cut clothes and held a medical bag in his large hands. And when he spoke there was a faint but distinct Scottish burr to his voice. "I understand that we may have three little ones with whooping cough." He looked at each of us in turn, no doubt trying to work out who was who.

"I am Constable Samuel Plank," I said, shaking his hand. "This is my wife, and Constable Wilson, and the innkeeper Mr Atkins. Two of the children are his, and the other is the daughter of a close friend. They are all upstairs."

"Then perhaps Mrs Plank will be so kind as to show me to their quarters," said Lockhart.

Martha looked surprised but led the physician from the parlour.

"He seems young," said Atkins.

"But competent," I replied. "You saw how he knew immediately that Martha would be of greatest use. And he is Mr Conant's personal physician. More importantly, he is Miss Lily's personal physician, and you can be certain that Mr Conant would permit only the finest to treat his daughter. Our little ones are in the best hands."

Twenty minutes later the innkeeper, Wilson and I were in the dining room, trying to distract ourselves by preparing tables for midday guests, when the physician sought us out. We pulled out chairs at a table for four and sat down.

"It is whooping cough," said Lockhart. "There is no doubt."

Atkins paled and gripped the back of a chair to steady himself.

"Mr Atkins," continued the physician, "much has been done recently to improve the treatment for whooping cough. A countryman of mine called Watts has made a study of the illness, looking at what causes it and – more importantly – what cures it. There is as yet no medicinal cure, but what we have learned is that the more traditional approaches – bleeding, sweating, vomiting and the like – have little effect except to weaken the patient.

Thankfully your wife and Miss Godfrey, through excellent maternal instincts, swiftly abandoned these harsh treatments. And under their tender care, it seems that Thomas is now past the crisis." Atkins dropped his head and took a sobbing breath. "He will be weak for some days," continued Lockhart, "but he will recover."

"And the girls?" I asked.

"Constable, I understand that you are particularly fond of the younger of the two girls," said the physician quietly. "And so you must prepare yourself. With the two lasses, their different ages are significant. Jane is nearly five, and her lungs and the muscles around them," here Lockhart indicated his own chest, "are stronger. This is important because the purpose of the cough is to expel matter from the lungs. Martha is only just two, and her cough weakens her more quickly and is less productive. I have shown all three ladies how to assist with the clearing of the lungs, and they already know about the importance of good food to build the strength. All we can do now is wait."

CHAPTER NINE

Surrounded by love

TUESDAY 5TH AUGUST 1828

The five days following my visit to the Blue Boar were among the hardest of my life. As a man, and as a constable, I am fitted for action and for putting things right. To be forced to wait because there was nothing to be done was a great test of my character – and I frequently found myself wanting, as I grew restive and lonely in the evenings and short-tempered during the days. Wilson and I walked to work as usual, perhaps a little quieter than normal, and when we did speak we avoided all mention of the monumental struggle that was taking place in the rooms above the Blue Boar. For her part, Martha all but lived at the inn, taking turns with Alice and Louisa Atkins to nurse the two little girls, and snatching a few hours' rest on a cot in the sick-room. I had to content myself with the bachelor life once again – a state I had been only too glad to abandon the first time round – and tried not to feel too sorry for myself as I lamented the temporary loss of all those womanly attentions that make a home.

On the sixth day after Martha had moved to Holborn I was just rinsing my plate after another uninspiring cold evening meal – a slice of pie donated by Thomas Neale's wife (a fierce woman but a gifted cook) and the heel of a plum loaf that I had been saving – when the back door opened and Martha walked in, followed by Wilson. One look at her stricken face told me everything. I opened my arms and she fell into them, beyond tears. I looked over her shoulder at Wilson.

"I had a warrant out Holborn way," he said, "and I carried on to the Blue Boar, for any news." He put the back of his big hand to first one eye and then the other. "Both gone. This afternoon. Mrs Plank was planning to stay, to sit with... with them. But I persuaded her to come home with me. We took a coach. She needs to sleep, sir."

"As do you, my lad," I said. I looked around the kitchen at the empty pots and bare plates, and then dug into my pocket for some coins and reached past Martha to hand them to Wilson. "That's for the coach. You go home now, and on the way use what's left to buy yourself something warming to eat. To eat, mind you – not to drink. Drink will do you no good when your spirits are already low."

Wilson took the coins and nodded his thanks. He hesitated a second or two before putting a hand on Martha's shoulder. Then he nodded again at me and left.

It was like undressing a doll. Martha stood, uncomplaining and unmoving, as I undid laces and hooks, lifted arms and feet, folded clothes and shook out a nightdress before pulling it on over her head. Even then she seemed uncertain what to do until I held up the bedclothes for her. She climbed in wordlessly and sat upright against the pillow, waiting for me to tuck in the bedding around her and then take the pins from her hair. Here my clumsiness was too much for her to tolerate, and she finished the task herself, dropping the pins one by one into my open palm. This done, she lay down, staring at the ceiling. I quickly undressed and slipped into bed alongside her, holding up my arm so that she could rest her head on my chest. I was relieved when she did so; a silent, distant Martha was an unfamiliar creature. I stroked her arm.

"Why is God so cruel?" she whispered. "Why does He let blameless children suffer?" I said nothing; they were not questions that expected an answer. "It was awful, Sam. To see them gasping for breath. Coughing fits that could turn you inside out. And then all of that stops. We thought the crisis was over – like with Thomas. But I could tell that Dr Lockhart was still worried." Martha turned her head to look up at me. "He came twice a day,

Sam. An important man like that, and twice a day he called on us. And he told me the signs to look for, signs that… that it was getting worse. And first it was little Martha, and then Jane. The heart racing, like it wants to jump out of the chest. We couldn't get them to take any food, even the smallest mouthfuls of their favourite treats. The cook tried every morsel in his larder to tempt them, the baker sent sweet biscuits to soak in milk – everyone was so kind. And at the same time, they could hold nothing in – they were like babies again, wrapped in clouts." Martha's voice dropped to a whisper. "They wasted away, Sam. At the end, there was nothing left of their poor little bodies." I reached for her hand and squeezed it. "It was almost a relief to let them go, God forgive me for saying it." Martha took a deep, shuddering breath. "She died in Alice's arms, with me holding her hand. Our little Martha died surrounded by love."

I struggled to keep the tears from my voice. "And that is all anyone can hope, my dearest. To live in love and to die with love. You could have done no more."

I kept hold of Martha's hand and stroked it over and over again. I could almost feel her mind racing as the grief played its tricks of blame and despair. But she was exhausted, and the body must rest. And only once I had heard her breath steady, slow and deepen, so that I could be sure she was asleep, did I allow myself to weep silently for the enchanting little girl who had sat on my knee, tugged at my whiskers and called me Grandpapa Sam.

CHAPTER TEN

Two handkerchiefs

FRIDAY 8TH AUGUST 1828

Three days later we gathered in the burial ground of St Dunstan in the West on Fleet Street. We were a small and heartbroken band: George and Louisa Atkins standing on either side of George's mother, and then Alice and Martha clutching each other with Wilson and me flanking them protectively. The grief was apparent in the blankness of Alice's face; even her red hair, always at odds with her quiet nature, seemed paler and less vibrant. Martha had told me that Alice had all but stopped eating, and her tiny frame reminded me of the day when I had found her and brought her into our lives – the day that little Martha was born.

I cannot bear to recall what I felt as the two small coffins were lowered into the ground, and I do not care to recall what crumbs of Christian comfort were offered by the clergyman. As the final prayer was said, a movement at the edge of the burial ground caught my eye and I looked up to see John Wontner replacing his hat. I left Martha with Wilson and Alice and walked over to him.

He shook my hand solemnly. "I was more sorry than I can say to hear about the little ones," he said. "Grace asked me to give these to the mothers. One for each of them." He handed me two flat parcels, wrapped in paper and tied with narrow ribbons – one yellow and one white. I looked up at him. "Handkerchiefs," he explained. "The yellow one is for Mrs Atkins and the white for Alice." He put his hand on my arm. "I am truly sorry, Sam, for them, and for you and Martha." He bowed his head and then walked away.

I returned to the mourning party and gave the little parcels to the women. They unwrapped them and inside were, as Wontner had said, two fine handkerchiefs, embroidered with a careful hand and an artist's eye. On one was the letter J and on the other an M, both twined about with delicate daisies and leaves.

"Daisies for innocence," said Martha quietly.

CHAPTER ELEVEN

Sunday meetings

SUNDAY 7TH SEPTEMBER 1828

It was many years since grief had entered our lives, and I had forgotten how it touches everything. Each morning I would wake and, for a second or two, all seemed normal. And then I would remember. But worse was waking before Martha and having to see the same realisation cross her face. I will admit that on some days I crept from our bed in the small hours and dozed in my armchair downstairs, simply so that I could avoid seeing the pain in her eyes as she recalled that little Martha was gone.

And so it was perhaps not surprising that Martha turned elsewhere for comfort. The prayer meetings that she had attended irregularly before now became a fixed and unmissable part of her week. The coal man – the grandson of Mrs Wilkes – would call round on Sunday mornings, I would help Martha up onto the bench of his cart beside him, and off they would go, Martha raising a hand in farewell as they turned the corner. Once she asked whether I would like to go with them – Fred Wilkes, she explained, did not come to the meeting himself but went to the Birdcage for a pint, and perhaps I could join him. After the meeting the four of them would have a picnic, and I was welcome to join them.

"The four of you?" I asked.

"Yes: Mrs Wilkes, Fred, Alice and me," said Martha, checking the contents of her basket and tucking a cloth in around them. "Mrs Wilkes is Fred's only family – she looked after him when he was small – and he likes to visit her every week. He's a nice fellow, Sam."

It was the first time that Martha had mentioned that Alice attended the meetings. I wondered whether she also went to the evening meetings that Martha now occasionally attended. I was uneasy about her going to them – no man likes to think of his wife out unaccompanied and unprotected after dark – but she did not invite me to go with her. And if they gave her some comfort at this bleak time, I did not want to press the matter. I had my work to occupy my mind, and if spending time listening to preachers did the same for her, I was grateful for that.

"How is Alice?" I asked, holding Martha's shawl, ready to wrap it around her shoulders.

Martha paused and looked at me. "She's young – still only seventeen – and, God willing, she will have more children." Martha had started referring to the Almighty more often these days. "But she seems lost, Sam. Louisa and George do their best, of course, but they have their own grief to bear. I tried to persuade her to come and stay here for a while, where we can keep an eye on her, but she says that Louisa needs her, and I daresay she does." Martha turned her back to me and I draped the shawl around her, kissing the nape of her neck as I did so. She looked round at me and smiled – it was the first smile I had seen on her face for weeks, and the sadness in it tore at my heart.

CHAPTER TWELVE

Just over two pounds

THURSDAY 18TH SEPTEMBER 1828

Some days later I was sitting in the back office of Great Marlborough Street, staring unseeing at a newspaper that had been left there the previous evening, when there was a knock at the door and Tom Neale looked in.

"Friend of yours here to see you – a Mr Atkins," said the office keeper. "Shall I bring him through? Looks like he needs a stiff drink, if I'm honest, but tea will have to do."

I nodded and Tom disappeared. A moment later the door opened again and in came George Atkins, looking somewhat diminished out of his natural surroundings, and with dark shadows smudged beneath his eyes. We shook hands and he sat down heavily into the chair I indicated.

"How are you, George?" I asked. I tried to keep the sympathy out of my voice – not because I didn't feel it, but because he had come to see me in my place of work and I sensed that I could serve him best as a constable, not as a friend.

He straightened his shoulders and put his hands on the table. "As well as can be expected, Sam. Easier for me than for Louisa, of course: if I stay on my feet and keep moving, keep working, I can stop thinking. There's little to beat a coaching inn for distraction. But if I sit down and start to think, well." He shook his head.

The door opened and Tom brought in the usual battered tray with mismatched cups and a pot of tea coddled in a cloth. He put it on the table, nodded at us both, and left.

"The tea is better than it appears," I said, pouring two cups. "It gets worse later in the day." I pushed a cup across the table to the innkeeper, who picked it up with both hands and sipped. He raised an eyebrow and nodded.

"Not bad at all," he said. He took another sip and then put the cup down and clasped his hands together. "Sam, I have come to see you about Alice. No, don't worry," he said hurriedly – he must have seen something on my face, "she's not unwell. Not physically unwell," he corrected himself.

I reached over to my coat hanging on the wall and extracted my notebook from the pocket. I opened it and looked enquiringly at George, and he nodded.

He took a deep breath and then said, "Alice has been stealing from us."

I will admit that it was not what I was expecting to hear. "Alice? Are you sure?" I asked.

"I know: it seems unlikely. But I saw her with my own eyes," he said sadly. "I saw her take money from the till. On two occasions. Tuesday morning, and then yesterday evening. That's when I decided to come and see you."

"To report the matter?" I asked.

"Oh no," said the innkeeper decisively. "I have no interest in recovering the money or punishing the poor girl. What I want to know is why she is doing it – what she needs the money for." He shook his head as though to clear it. "Alice has lived with us for more than two years now, and not once during all that time has she done anything like this. She never took so much as a slice of bread without asking. She has her board and lodging with us, as you know, and little Martha did too," he sniffed but continued, "and Louisa gave her a bit of money each week for, well, whatever women spend their money on." He shrugged and looked at me, and I shrugged in sympathy. "So why does she suddenly need more?"

"What does Mrs Atkins think?" I asked.

"Oh, I haven't told Louisa," he said quickly. "She has enough on her plate at the minute, and she and Alice, well, they need each other, I think. Who better to understand than another grieving mother? I cannot separate them now."

Wilson's jaw dropped. "Alice?" he repeated. "Stealing?" He sat back in his chair.

I wondered once again whether I should have mentioned the matter to him, but I needed his help. I had already decided not to tell Martha, as I did not want her to be more concerned about Alice than she already was, and Wilson could be useful. He had been very fond of little Martha and had often spent his half-day with her and her mother. Alice was far more likely to talk to Wilson than she was to confide in me.

"But why? How much?" he spluttered.

"Just over two pounds, according to Mr Atkins," I said. "A few half-crowns, some shillings and the rest in pennies."

"No notes or sovereigns?" Wilson asked. I knew what he was thinking: the smaller coins were easier to spend without arousing suspicion, and might not be noticed missing.

I shook my head. "And it might be more. Mr Atkins started seeing a shortfall in his cashing up about three weeks ago. Everyone at the inn has worked for him for a year or more, so he didn't suspect any of them..."

"And an inn is a busy place," said Wilson hotly. "Full of people coming and going – strangers at all hours. If the till was left unwatched, or maybe Mr Atkins counted up wrong..." His voice tailed off as he saw me shaking my head.

"Mr Atkins was in the small room behind the parlour – you know the one," I said. Wilson nodded. "The curtain was across the doorway, but he heard someone come in and walk behind the counter. The floorboard there squeaks, he said. He pulled the curtain aside just enough to see, and it was Alice. He saw her open the drawer and take some coins out and put them into her pocket."

"But he didn't stop her," said Wilson. It was an observation, not a question.

"He did not," I confirmed. "Mr Atkins is not concerned about the money, he says. He does not want to punish Alice, or even let her know that he knows. What he wants is to understand why she is doing it." I looked at Wilson. "Do you know why Alice would need money?"

"I know Mrs Atkins gives her some every week, and Alice told me that she was saving it for little Martha." We were both silent for a moment. "When we went out, we didn't spend much: Alice always brought food from the inn, and sometimes I'd buy them a cake or a little toy." He looked at me with such sadness on his open face. "She is an honest girl, sir. Whatever it is, it must be terrible to make her do this."

I cleared my throat. "Now then, lad, we don't want to jump to conclusions. Alice is very young still, and the young sometimes make rash decisions. It might be foolish rather than terrible. Like that time you considered buying that evening cape."

Wilson flushed. "I did not consider buying it," he said hotly. "I just looked at it in the shop window."

"As you wish," I said.

"So you think Alice might be buying fancy items?" he asked.

"Do you?" I replied. "You see her more often than I do. Has her manner of dress changed? Her scent? Her hair?"

He shook his head. "Alice is too sensible for all that," he said.

"I agree," I said. "But the fact remains that she is taking money for some purpose – some purpose for which her regular funds are inadequate. Some purpose that she cannot confess to Mr and Mrs Atkins – or to you – in order to ask openly for more money. And we need to find out what that purpose is, so that we can help her."

"A warrant?" asked Mr Conant. He was at his table, reading and signing papers.

I nodded. "I know it is an unusual request, sir, but I cannot think of any other way. May I?" I indicated the empty chair at the table; the magistrate nodded and I sat down. "I have just had a visit from George Atkins, the innkeeper at the Blue Boar. He has seen Alice Godfrey taking money from the till."

Conant looked surprised. "Your young mother?"

"Yes, sir," I said. "He does not want to bring her before the law, but wishes simply to understand why she is in need of money. She has recently lost her child, as you know," the magistrate shook his head sadly, "and as a consequence is perhaps not herself." I leaned forward. "Mrs Plank was very fond of the little girl." I took a deep breath. "As was I. But I have my work to occupy me, and for that I am thankful. Since our bereavement, Mrs Plank has found consolation in attending gatherings – religious gatherings – at Cooper's Gardens."

"Cooper's Gardens?" repeated Conant. "That sounds familiar. Ah: that is where Mr Welford and his wife worshipped, is it not? The man who smothered his wife in their bed?"

"It is, yes, sir," I replied. "And a few days ago Martha – Mrs Plank – told me that Alice attends these meetings as well. I cannot – I dare not – quiz my wife about what happens at these gatherings. She would think that I am doubting her judgement."

Conant look at me for a long moment. "And so you seek to discuss the matter with Mr Welford instead."

"I do, yes, if that would be permitted," I said.

The magistrate reached for a piece of paper. "You may not get much sense from the fellow," he said as he dipped his pen into the ink pot. "He was found guilty but insane, remember."

CHAPTER THIRTEEN

Bethlem

FRIDAY 19TH SEPTEMBER 1828

"Guilty but insane?" asked Wilson as we walked along Westminster Bridge Road. I noticed that his usual smart pace had slowed as we neared our destination.

"Aye," I said. "As you know, Welford pleaded guilty from the start. A hearing was held simply to establish the facts of the matter, and at that hearing he confirmed that he knew that killing his wife was wrong. But thankfully for him – otherwise it would have been a trip to the scaffold – he said enough to convince the judge that although he should be held responsible for his actions, he was not completely right in the head. And since a law passed in, I think, 1800, we have had benefit of a verdict of 'guilty but insane'. And for this the punishment is not death as it would be for sane murderers, but rather to be kept in a place of custody until His Majesty's pleasure be known. For those found guilty but insane in London, that place of custody is here in Bethlem."

Wilson's pace slowed even more. "Are they all, well, raving, do you think?" he asked.

"As I understand it," I said as I paused to cross the street, "this is one of the most advanced lunatic hospitals in the world. There will probably be some inmates – some patients – who are raving, but equally there will be others who are quiet, and others who are lost in their own imaginary worlds."

Although I tried to speak with confidence, I had a certain sympathy with Wilson's unease. Physical deformity is familiar: you know what to expect of a man who is blind or lame. But disease of the mind is less predictable, and as such more unsettling. We turned into St George's Fields, and New Bethlem Hospital rose before us in all its majesty. It was quite a building: only twenty years old, it was nearly six hundred feet in length, with a central domed block flanked by two wings of three storeys – one wing for men and the other for women. Surrounded by a tall brick wall with a central section of railings giving views onto extensive grounds within, it looked more like a grand country estate than a madhouse.

We walked to the main entrance gate and I rang the bell. After showing the warrant signed by Mr Conant, we were escorted through the magnificent columned portico into the central hall of the building. The man who had walked with us from the gate indicated that we should wait while he disappeared into a side room with the warrant. He returned a minute later and beckoned us to follow him.

"Come," he said. "Stay close. We have to walk through the male gallery to reach the criminal wing. The patients are at leisure at the moment and may approach us. The truly dangerous are not allowed to wander at will, of course, but they are all unpredictable to one degree or another." He looked back to check our faces. "You will have seen much worse, I am sure, constables, but it is as well to be careful."

And indeed I have seen much worse. Once we had passed through the locked doors that signalled the start of the male wing of the building, we could have been in a gentlemen's club, or perhaps a seminary. Tall windows – albeit barred – allowed light to flood into the long gallery. Men of all ages and mostly unremarkable were walking about, or sitting in chairs, or gathered about tables, and engaged in all manner of activities – reading, playing cards, deep in discussion, and there was even one teaching a spaniel to sit for its ball. Hanging baskets of greenery gave the place an air of homeliness, while busts and other ornaments graced niches and shelves that broke up the space between the windows. As we walked along the gallery, some of the men looked at us and one or two called a greeting to the keeper, but the majority simply ignored us.

"There is a separate wing for noisy patients," said the keeper. "The facilities there are not as congenial as in this gallery, and the men quickly learn that kicking up a fuss lands them in those less pleasant surroundings. Talking of which..."

We came to the end of the gallery. To our right was another light and airy space – "the day room" explained the keeper – but we turned left down a darker and narrower corridor. I glanced in through an open door and saw two bath tubs, each fully covered by a wooden lid so that all you could see of the occupant was his head. Wilson followed my gaze and shivered. We walked on until we reached a heavy door on which the keeper knocked. A small window in the door was opened at eye-level and the keeper spoke to his counterpart on the other side and then posted my warrant through the window.

"I will hand you over now to Mr Earling; he is the attendant in charge of the male criminal wing," said the keeper. "Goodbye, constables." He waited until the door had been opened, we had both walked through it and it had been fastened securely once again. We caught a last glimpse of him as the little window in the door was slid shut again by Mr Earling.

"So you're wanting a word with our Mr Welford," said Earling chattily as he read the warrant again. "Let me just make a note of all the particulars and I will take you directly to him." The attendant went into a small office off the corridor and sat at a desk. He pulled a large ledger towards him and started to write in it, glancing from it to the warrant and back again. "Which is Plank and which is Wilson?" he asked as he dipped his pen.

"I am Constable Plank," I replied.

He looked up at me. "About five foot four inches tall?" he asked.

"Precisely," I agreed. "Why do you need that for your ledger?"

"We have to keep a careful record of everyone on the wing, in case of impersonation. In the past, patients have waylaid visitors, taken their clothes, and left the hospital. And of course if there is any violence, we need to be able to identify the victims quickly. Five foot ten, Constable Wilson?"

Wilson nodded. I could see that he was unsettled by the attendant's talk of violence. "But Mr Welford has shown no signs of violence?" I asked quickly.

The attendant blew on the ledger page to dry the ink and stood. "That one? Heavens, no – mild as a mouse. But quite gone in the mind, of course. One minute he's telling you how he murdered his wife, and the next he's asking you to get word to her that he'll be late home." He joined us in the corridor and glanced up at a clock on the wall. "They'll be in the airing ground now; do you want to talk to him there, or shall I bring him back to his sleeping room?"

"The airing ground, please," said Wilson urgently, taking me by surprise. "I could do with some air myself."

The airing ground for the criminally insane men was well-used, with about forty men outside watched over by three attendants. Some men were simply sitting on the grass, others were gathered in standing groups, and there was a lively game of trap-ball going on in one corner, with players shouting encouragement and abuse at each other just as you would find in any schoolyard or playing field. Earling looked around and then pointed to a bench under a tree.

"There, that's Mr Welford," he said. "He's not the most sociable of men, but he's no bother – keeps himself to himself. I'll leave you to it, and when you want to leave, let one of the attendants know and he'll escort you out." Earling raised a hand in farewell to the attendants, who acknowledged him with a nod, and then he returned indoors.

Wilson and I walked over to Welford, who watched us without curiosity.

"May I?" I asked, indicating the space beside him on the bench.

"Of course, sir," said Welford, and I sat.

"It is a fine day for September," I observed. My companion glanced up at the sky and nodded but said nothing. "Do you remember me, Mr Welford?" I asked.

He looked at me. "I do," he said. "You're the constable who came to see me after I killed Rose."

"Your wife, that's right," I said. "You said that they had told you to do it, if you recall."

"They did, that's right," he agreed.

"Who did, Mr Welford?" I asked.

"My brethren," he said as though I should have known.

"At Cooper's Gardens?" I asked.

He shook his head.

"Where, then?" I asked.

"At the vinegar yard," he said.

"The vinegar yard?" I asked. "Which vinegar yard?"

"The one on City Road," he replied. "Where we have our meetings."

"Do the same brethren go to both places – Cooper's Gardens and the vinegar yard?" I asked.

"A few of us go to both, but not many. We were chosen," he said with pride. "Chosen for our true faith."

I looked up at Wilson, pleased to see that he had his notebook in his hand and was writing carefully. Even a large constable like Wilson can seem invisible if he keeps still and says nothing, and Welford made no sign of even having noticed him.

"Who chose you, Mr Welford?" I asked.

He looked at me as though I was a simpleton. "Why, God of course, constable!"

"Of course," I said. "And who told you that God had chosen you?"

"One of the brethren," he said. "Came up to me in Cooper's Gardens, when I was setting off home, and said that I should go to the next meeting at the vinegar yard. Held every Wednesday."

"And Mrs Welford – was she chosen too?" I asked.

He shook his head sadly. "Rose did not see what I saw; her ears were not open to the message. She came to Cooper's Gardens once but said that it was not right, that God would not heed us if we were not in a church." He turned to me and clutched my arm. "I fear for her soul, constable. I pray that she is given the blessing of eternal salvation in the blessed arms of God." He let go of my arm and clasped his hands together.

"And so you went alone to a meeting at the vinegar yard?" I asked.

"I went to many meetings there," he said. "They even asked me to stand with the collection bag."

"And did you put money into the bag yourself, as well as collecting from others?" I asked.

"Of course," Welford replied indignantly. "How can we spread the word of salvation without funds?" And then his shoulders slumped and a look of great sadness came across his face. “But I could not give as much as I wanted. Rose would not permit it.”

I glanced up at Wilson and he raised an eyebrow. “And did that make you angry, Mr Welford? That she would not give you the money you asked for?”

He shook his head. “Not angry, no. But I felt helpless, that I could not give enough. I explained my situation to the brethren, and they said that they understood. They were sympathetic. They said that a man with such devotion would be welcome at one of their special meetings.” He looked off into the distance for a few moments. When he spoke again, his voice was even quieter. “And so, the evening before we met, you and I, constable, I went to a special meeting. Just me and a few of the brethren, and the herald.”

“Where was this special meeting, Mr Welford?” I asked.

He shrugged. “I was taken there,” he said. “It was not far from the vinegar yard – a house. A tall house.” His voice became excited. “And there was a message for me, just as they had promised. The herald had a message for me.”

“The herald?” I asked. “What is a herald?”

“The herald is the one who delivers the messages, at the Wednesday meetings,” Welford explained patiently. “I’ve heard her deliver messages from a woman to her husband, and from a grandmother to her grandson. One meeting was very affecting, when woman who had longed for a child for more than ten years was told that a baby would be born within a twelvemonth. How she cried with joy to hear that, constable!" He paused with a beatific smile on his face at the recollection.

"And your message?" I prompted.

"Mine was not so pleasant, but then the messages tell you what you need to hear, and not just what you want to hear," he explained. "My message came from my own dear mother, dead these twenty years. She said that Rose was wrong to stop me giving the money, and that the salvation of my eternal soul was the most important thing. She said that Heaven is a glorious place, and that she would be waiting for me. And then she said that if Rose was in my way, she was being controlled by the Devil, and that I should kill her to halt his advance."

"Did that surprise you, Mr Welford?" I asked. "That your mother should tell you to kill your wife?"

He shrugged. "My mother was none too fond of Rose, but it was not revenge, if that is what you are thinking. Mother was thinking only of my salvation, and of Rose's soul." He looked at me. "I did it as gently as I could, constable. I waited until she was asleep. You saw her: peaceful, she looked. She made the ultimate sacrifice, and now we shall be united in Heaven, Rose and I." He smiled again.

"Did anyone at the meeting try to stop you, Mr Welford? Suggest that you should think again?" I asked.

Welford glanced at me in surprise. "Stop me killing Rose?" he asked. I nodded. "Why would they try to stop me? They heard what I heard. My instructions were quite clear, and the messages always know what must be done. My message was delivered when the most important brethren were there to hear it." He looked proud as he said this. "They knew what had to be done."

A bell started to clang somewhere in the hospital and all the men in the airing ground looked towards it, including Welford. "Dinner," he explained to us as he stood. "Would you excuse me, sir – they like us to be prompt."

"Of course," I said, standing as well. Welford started walking towards the door where men were gathering to be allowed back into the building. After a few steps he stopped and turned to look back at us.

"When you see Rose, sir," he said, "please would you tell her that I am well fed and cared for, but that I look forward to coming home soon." He shook his head and smiled sadly. "She's a good woman, and she worries about me, I know."

Wilson and I waited in the airing ground until all the patients had gone indoors and an attendant had completed his checks of the shed and the privy to make sure that no-one remained outside. He then ushered us ahead of him and locked the doors behind us as we retraced our steps through the hospital. The corridors and galleries were empty, with all the men presumably tucking into their food in a dining hall somewhere. The attendant read my thoughts and pointed upwards.

"They're up there," he said. "Fish on Fridays."

"It is early for dinner," I observed, checking a clock as we passed; it showed ten minutes past four.

"Settling the patients for bed is the hardest part of the job," explained the attendant. "Worse than babies, most of them. The sooner we start, the sooner we'll finish. And here we are, gentlemen." He unlocked a final door and stood aside to let us pass. We found ourselves back in the grand entrance hall. "You're in luck," he said, pointing at the opposite wall. "The curtains are open. You can pay your respects to our two friends." He then gave a single nod of farewell, stepped backwards and pulled the door closed between us.

We walked across the entrance hall. Heavy green silk curtains had been pulled aside and a small group of well-dressed visitors was looking at whatever had been revealed. Wilson – with a better view thanks to his height – took a sharp intake of breath.

"I know," said a woman, turning to me and then back again quickly so that the feather in her hat waved jauntily.

"Aren't they just awful? And yet one cannot stop looking." She shuddered and took hold of the arm of the man on her other side. "Awful," she repeated.

Set on low plinths in front of us were two reclining statues made of stone, their surface pitted and rough. The woman's companion looked around her to catch my eye.

"Portland stone," he said. "Carved by some Danish fellow in 1767. The one on the right," he pointed, "is called Raving Madness, while his companion," he pointed again, "is Melancholy Madness. Well-named, are they not?" The woman with the feather looked up at him admiringly and squeezed his arm.

I looked at the two statues. They were both life-sized, naked but for loincloths, and bald-headed. Raving Madness was chained to his plinth, a tortured expression on his face as he fought for release, while Melancholy Madness looked vacant and defeated. I wondered which Welford would eventually resemble.

CHAPTER FOURTEEN

A long way from home

WEDNESDAY 24TH SEPTEMBER 1828

The house was cold and quiet, and to be honest I was grateful to have an excuse to go out. Martha had left a note on the table, explaining that she had gone to one of her meetings. She did not say where it was, and so used was I to her former openness that I did not know how to ask her without sounding like either a jealous lover or a curious constable. As a consequence, these days more often than not she went her way and I went mine.

I turned over Martha's note and wrote on the back of it 'Out at work – back before midnight' before leaving it in the same place on the table. I took my coat from the hook and looked sadly around the kitchen before going out.

On our way home from Bethlem, Wilson and I had decided that we needed to find out more about the gatherings at the vinegar yard on Wednesdays. But two men arriving together would draw more attention, particularly when one of them was a big, strapping fellow, and I said that I would go alone. In truth, I was glad to avoid another evening of stilted conversation with Martha.

The briny aroma of vinegar was unmistakeable. For nearly thirty years there had been a vinegar yard at the corner of Old Street Road and City Road, sitting on the site of what had once been a brewery, and it was now an impressive concern. "Champion & Green" said the sign over the main entrance, although of course at this time of night the large gates were closed. A smaller gate alongside them, however, was not, and I tucked in behind a man and a woman as they entered, touching my hat in greeting. The man who had called the meeting must be either a trusted worker, I reflected, to be allowed to use the premises in this way, or able to grease the night watchman in the fist.

Once inside the yard I followed the couple to a door in the far corner. I had taken care to time my arrival to be among the last to arrive but not so late that people would notice me, and when we walked into the room someone was clapping his hands to call the meeting to order. I looked around. We were in a fairly large room furnished sparely with long tables and benches – it was obviously where the workers ate during their breaks – and I slid onto the end of a bench near the door. I placed my hat on the table in front of me but kept my coat collar turned up to hide as much of my face as I could without drawing attention to myself. I nodded a greeting to the man next to me and the woman opposite, and then the man who had been clapping started to talk.

"Brothers and sisters," he said in a strong voice that gave him away instantly as a country fellow, "you are very welcome. I see some faces that I know, and some new friends too." I deliberately kept my attention on the speaking man – I did not want to look around the room while others were doing the same. "For those I have yet to meet, my name is John Buxton."

Buxton was a handsome man of about forty, with dark curling hair. He had the broad-shouldered build of a man used to hard toil and – as far as I could tell from some distance – had yet to develop the belly that comes from a fondness for ale or soft living. He was wearing a plain brown coat and breeches, with the heavy boots of a labourer. He opened his arms wide. "Let us start with our prayer," he said, and bent his head. Although I rarely trouble God with my own requests and petitions, I am able to intone the Lord's Prayer as well as anyone and this

I did. I took this opportunity to look around the room. I do not know what I was expecting to see, but it was certainly not this: sitting two tables across from me and much nearer the front of the room was Alice. I shifted slightly on my bench to make sure that, should she glance my way, she would not spy me. But judging from the fixed fervour of her gaze upon Buxton once the prayer was finished, I doubted she would look anywhere but at him. Just then another woman, a shawl over her bonnet to protect her from the cool night air, squeezed her way between the seats until she reached Alice, and touched her on the shoulder. Alice shifted on the bench to let the new arrival sit down, and as this woman rearranged her shawl around her shoulders, it was all I could do not to call out, for it was Martha.

"Brother and sisters," said Buxton after the amen, "let us turn now to the business of our gathering." There was a general rustling as people adjusted their positions so that they could secure as clear a view as possible; Martha and Alice sat tight up against each other and gave each other a quick, excited look before turning their attention to Buxton. For his part, he walked to the side of the room and held out his hand to a woman seated on a chair against the wall; she stood and accompanied him to the front, keeping hold of his hand as she stepped up onto a wooden crate that had been placed there for her. She was a slight little thing, a few years older than Alice, dressed in sombre colours and with a woollen shawl gathered about her. She was pale, her fair hair tucked away under her bonnet and her blue eyes large in her face. And when she stood upright on the crate, it was plain to all that she was heavily pregnant.

"Although she approaches her confinement," said Buxton, "Eliza has come here this evening as herald because she has news for some of you." I could feel the expectation in the air; the woman opposite me put a hand on her heart and the man next to her – her husband, I assumed – laid a comforting hand on her shoulder. Buxton held up a hand. "Not all of you, not by any means, but some of you, yes." He turned to Eliza and she bent to whisper in his ear. "Hester Woodman," he intoned.

There was a gasp from a woman a few seats down from me and she raised her hand. I could see that it was trembling.

"Stand if you would, Hester," said Buxton. The woman did as he asked. He turned back to Eliza. "Is this the woman you seek?" he asked her. Eliza closed her eyes and put her head a little to one side, as though listening for something in the distance. We waited in silence for perhaps half a minute until Eliza opened her eyes and nodded. "And what message have you for Hester?" asked Buxton.

"You are a widow," said Eliza. She spoke softly, in the artificial tone I hear Martha use when she is nervous –

her society voice, I call it. Although it had not been a question, the woman Hester nodded vigorously. "Your late husband was a porter – no, I misheard – a slaughter man."

"He was," agreed Mrs Woodman. "At Smithfield."

Eliza nodded. "That is why he is wearing an apron, then."

Several people gasped and looked around the room, craning their necks to see what Eliza could see. I myself glanced around, but whatever else was there I certainly did not expect to see a dead slaughter man clad in his bloodied apron. His widow put her hand to her mouth and nodded.

"He speaks," said Eliza. She put her head on one side again, listening carefully, and then nodded. "He says that you are not to marry the man who has asked you. He says that this man will not care for you."

"Oh!" said Mrs Woodman in surprise.

"Is this true?" asked Buxton. "Hester, has someone asked you to marry him?"

I looked down the bench towards the widow. Mrs Woodman was clutching the edge of the table.

"It is true," she said in wonderment. She looked around the room. "William has been gone these eighteen months, and only last week a man I have known for many years asked me to marry him. A friend of William's, from the market. A widower. A good man, I thought, but I was not sure enough of my answer – I asked for time to think."

"It is as well you did," said Buxton approvingly. "No doubt William knew of your uncertainty, and seeks to guide you."

"It must be," said the woman opposite me to her husband. "He comes back to protect her." The husband caught my eye and lifted his shoulders in a shrug.

Buxton spoke again. "Does William have anything more to say to Hester?" he asked Eliza.

The young woman closed her eyes again and waited. A few moments later she said, "He is pleased to see that you are among friends."

I looked again at the widow. She nodded fervently. "Oh, I am – indeed I am," she said.

"And now he has gone," concluded Eliza.

The widow Woodman sat down, and those around her leaned in excitedly towards her. I looked over to Martha and Alice; my wife had her arm around the young woman, and Alice's head was on Martha's shoulder.

Buxton waited for a moment, looking towards the widow and smiling, and then spoke. "Brothers and sisters, as you know, these meetings take their toll on Eliza. While she rests and regains her strength – for she tells me that there are others for whom she has messages – we will sit in silent prayer and reflection."

He held his hand out to Eliza and she stepped down from the crate and was escorted back to her chair. There she leaned her head against the wall and closed her eyes. Buxton took his place again at the front of the room and bowed his head. My neighbours and I did likewise. My mind was racing as I considered what I could say to Martha and Alice at the end of the meeting, but after a few seconds my thoughts were interrupted. I felt someone standing at my shoulder; for a moment I feared it was Martha, but then a man leaned down and whispered into my ear, "You're a long way from Great Marlborough Street, Constable Plank".

CHAPTER FIFTEEN

Riding out the storm

THURSDAY 25TH SEPTEMBER 1828

Martha was quiet again at breakfast the next morning. She had arrived home before me the previous evening and taken herself to bed; I had not woken her on my return, but had simply curved my night-chilled body around her warm one and spent a restless night turning things over in my mind. When I am troubled it is Martha to whom I turn for advice or humour or – when all else fails – comfort. And when she is taken from me, I am a poor specimen. I longed to know why she had been at the vinegar yard meeting, but she and Alice had seemed so contented together with their shared adventure – if Buxton's meetings brought them peace, and Martha chose not to tell me about them, what damage might I do by prying? I am a constable, yes, but before that I am a husband.

"Will you be out this evening?" I asked as I put on my coat.

"Just because I spend some evenings away from home," Martha replied tartly, "there is no reason to suppose that I am going to leave you to shift for yourself all the time."

"I did not mean that," I protested. "I asked simply to know your plans."

"And your plans, Sam," she replied. "Do you always tell me your plans?"

I knew that whatever I said I would be in the wrong, and it saddened me because Martha is not by nature a contrary or argumentative woman. We have lively discussions, certainly, and what she calls 'differences of opinion', and on occasion we have said hurtful and cutting things to each other. But she is not one of those sharp creatures who prod and provoke, and consequently I am not one of those men who know how to protect themselves from such spikes.

I walked over to my wife and bent to kiss her on the cheek, which she permitted but did not welcome.

"Take care of yourself, my dear," I said.

She nodded, and lifted her chin in defiance of the tears shining in her eyes.

Tom Neale looked at me from behind his counter and frowned with concern. He waved some papers at the young constable sitting on the bench against the wall.

"Here you are, lad – work your way through those," he said. "You can read them as you walk," he added. "Constable Plank and I have important matters to discuss."

The constable huffed a bit at the thought of being turned out of the warm office but he clapped his hat on his head and left us.

"Back office," said Tom. "Tea."

Minutes later he joined me in the back room and put his battered tray on the table. He handed me a cup and sat down with his own, sipping it and smacking his lips in appreciation.

"Work or women?" he asked.

"Both," I said.

"In that case," he said, lifting the cloth he had draped over a plate on the tray, "it is as well that my good wife made these yesterday. And even better that she was too busy shouting at me this morning to notice me slipping a few into my pocket." He gestured to the plate. "Shortbread. She's a foul-tempered woman but a marvellous cook, and I stay for the latter and keep out of the way of the former." He winked at me. "Mrs Plank, on the other hand, is both sweet-tempered and handy in the kitchen, is she not?" He raised an eyebrow at me as he broke his piece of shortbread in half and then dabbed at the crumbs on the table with his finger.

"She was," I said miserably. "The food is still good, that is, but the sweetness, well…"

"Ah," said Tom. Like all who deal with human frailty every day, he knew when to speak and when to stay silent and let the confessions come at their own pace.

"Last night I went to a meeting – a religious meeting," I said. If Tom was surprised at the turn in the conversation, he did not show it. "Charlie Gordon was there."

"Charlie Gordon?" he repeated with a bark of laughter. "Now there's a rogue I haven't seen for many years. Thieving was his game, wasn't it – even with that withered arm. Has he turned parson, then?"

"No, not Charlie," I said, smiling despite myself. "After the meeting he followed me outside. He started to tell me all about how he had been called to God, but I can spot a yarn as well as he can spin one, and I told him so. He laughed then, and showed me a cloth bag: he said that they stand in the yard after the meetings and collect money from people as they are leaving."

"Isn't it more usual to pass the collection plate inside, during the service?" asked Tom, pointing to the shortbread. I took another piece; Mrs Neale was indeed an excellent cook.

"At a traditional church service, yes," I said. "But these meetings are a bit less… established." I looked at Tom and sighed. "People attend them in the hopes of hearing messages from their departed loved ones – words from beyond the grave."

"Indeed," said Tom. "And were you hoping for a message yourself?"

"Of course not," I said. "But I know some who do believe that it is possible – or maybe they simply hope that it is possible." I paused for a few moments. "Charlie Gordon said that those people at the meeting who have heard these messages are particularly generous afterwards."

"So is it just a way to trim people, do you think?" asked Tom.

"That was my first thought," I agreed, "but at the meeting last night the herald – that's what they call the woman who claims she can deliver messages from the departed – said things that are hard to explain."

"Such as?" prompted Tom.

I told him about the widow and what Eliza had said to her. "And Eliza's message was accurate," I finished. "Mrs Woodman told us that she had been considering remarriage, and to a friend of her late husband. How could Eliza have known that?"

Tom smiled. "It's obvious that you're no expert in women, Sam." He leaned forward. "Tell me: can you imagine a woman – any woman – receiving a marriage proposal, and not telling her friend, or her sister, or her mother?" I shook my head. "Of course not. News like that travels fast – women do love a celebration. And with a few paid ears listening at the right doors, it's not hard to find out about people's private business."

I thought back to exactly what Eliza had said, and actually it was very little: it was Mrs Woodman herself who had told us the name of her suitor, and had explained his relationship to her late husband. The herald had simply echoed her.

"And from the sound of it, if Charlie Gordon is to be believed, it's a clever little trick," said Tom. "If this Mrs Woodman thinks that her husband is still watching over her and giving her advice, she'll go to more meetings to hear from him again, and put more money into that cloth bag."

Thanks to either Tom's rational thinking or his wife's invigorating shortbread, the fog in my brain had lifted. "And I'll bet they play it both ways," I said. "If Mrs Woodman's new fellow hears that the messages are warning her against him, he might pay a fair bit himself to stop them."

"Devious, that is," said Tom. Just then a shout came from the front office and Tom stood up. "No peace for the wicked, eh, Sam?" He put our cups back onto the tray and then paused. "Now that we've sorted that out, are you any clearer on what to do about Mrs Plank?"

I shook my head.

"Ah well," said Tom, opening the door, "I doubt I could have helped with that. Keep your head down and ride out the storm – that's the only wisdom I can offer when it comes to wives."

CHAPTER SIXTEEN

Religious instruction

FRIDAY 26TH SEPTEMBER 1828

"It is a pleasure, as always, to see you, Sam," said Edward Freame with a smile. The banker and I had first met a few years earlier, when I was struggling to decipher banking records, and I had quickly come to respect and like him, and indeed often had cause to call on his expertise, which was always generously and willingly shared. We had become more closely connected the previous year, when Freame had recruited Martha to assist with the education of young girls at a school he had founded with a group of fellow Quakers. "But you are not your usual cheerful self today," he observed. "Come and take your ease: I can leave the ledgers until later." He closed the book on his lap and placed it on the floor beside his chair. "Now, how can I be of help?"

"I find myself troubled about religion," I said hesitatingly.

"Religion?" repeated the banker. "Has it come to this, Sam? Are you feeling the chill breath of mortality, and fear for your soul?" His teasing tone made light of his words.

"Yes, but no," I said. "I am no longer a young man, that's true, but my soul will have to take its own chances. I mean religion in theory rather than in practice." I took a deep breath. "A few nights ago I went to a gathering of Methodists. What I saw at that meeting is concerning me. And if anyone can help me to understand those new religions, it is you."

The banker leaned back in his chair and gave me a level look. "Quakerism is hardly a new religion, Sam; it is nearly two centuries since Mr Fox first preached our principles."

"I meant no offence, Edward," I said hurriedly. "I simply suggest that you have thought about these things more deeply. For my own part, as you know, I hold that God is unlikely to have truck with the pettiness of the church. Why would an Almighty Being concern Himself with who eats what on which days, and whether the right words are said at the right place in a service written by men?"

Freame smiled and shook his head. "I trust that you do not express these forthright opinions to all and sundry, Sam."

"Only to those who recognise reasoned debate when they hear it," I replied.

There was a knock on the parlour door and a lanky young man came into the room.

"You remember Stevenson, I am sure," said the banker.

"Good afternoon, Constable Plank," said Stevenson, giving a small bow.

"I see that you have been promoted, Stevenson," I said, indicating the ink-stains on his hands.

Stevenson flushed. "I have, sir, yes. Mr Harris is teaching me the ledgers, and in quieter moments I copy them out in order to learn the double entry system. I am not yet allowed to write in the new ledgers." He held out his hands. "I try not to make smudges, but they do seem to follow me."

Freame smiled encouragingly. "They follow you because you are impatient – as indeed a young man should be. Once you learn to take your time, the ink will dry, and your work will become neater. Mr Harris's work is neat only because he is a fellow of great age – a senior clerk – and has learned great patience."

"Thank you, sir," said Stevenson. "I shall try harder." He started to leave and then remembered that he had called on us. "I came to ask if you would like some tea, sir – you and Constable Plank."

"That would be most welcome, Stevenson, thank you. Oh, and make a cup for yourself, and one for Mr Harris as well. And I think there may be four jam tartlets in here – Mrs Freame had her weekly battle with the rolling pin yesterday." The banker reached under his seat and handed a small tin to the clerk, who smiled broadly and left the parlour.

"I swear that boy can sniff out a pastry at five hundred yards," said Freame with a smile. "He thinks I haven't noticed, but he offers to make the tea only on days when that tin comes to work with me."

A few minutes later, after Stevenson had returned with our tea tray – and a tell-tale smudge of jam on his lip – we resumed our discussion of religion. I told the banker about the two meetings: first the one I had gone to with Martha at Cooper's Gardens, and then the one I had attended alone at the vinegar yard. He listened carefully to my descriptions of the locations and the content of the meetings.

"The gathering in Cooper's Gardens," he said when I had finished, "sounds like many others taking place up and down the country led by a certain sort of Methodist. Ranters, they are sometimes called," I nodded, "although I think that does them a disservice. From all accounts, they do very little ranting and speak much sense. But when confronted with a new way of doing things – a way that challenges our long-practiced habits – we often reach for pejorative terms."

"Quakers, for instance," I said mischievously. "Trembling in the way of the Lord."

"Indeed, Sam," said Freame with a smile. He dabbed a finger at the crumbs left on his plate. "And this Reverend Miller you heard. I know the name; he is well-regarded."

I nodded. "I can believe it. He spoke well. As did his wife, according to Martha."

Freame raised an eyebrow. "Allowing women to preach – whatever next. Who knows: you might end up with another Mrs Fry."

The name of Elizabeth Fry was familiar to me: John Wontner, keeper of Newgate, had often spoken to me in glowing terms of the compassionate work done by this Quaker lady preacher, who campaigned and toiled so energetically for reform in the treatment of female prisoners.

The banker continued. "But this second meeting, that sounds an altogether more peculiar event. What did you say was the name of that preacher?"

"John Buxton," I replied.

Freame thought for a moment and then shook his head. "No: I have not heard of him. And this bringing up of the girl to the front, the herald, and the – the messages, you say?" I nodded. "To be honest, Sam, that sounds more like something you might pay to see in a tent at the Bartholomew Fair."

"Indeed," I said. "That was my view too. Particularly when Charlie Gordon appeared at the same meeting." I drained my cup. "A scoundrel I have known for years. He tried to convince me that he had seen the error of his ways, but all Charlie has ever seen is how to line his own pocket. So you are of the view that Mr Buxton's methods do not tally with any legitimate religious movement?"

Freame shook his head. "None of which I am aware, Sam." I considered telling him that Martha had attended the meeting, but it seemed disloyal; it was one thing for me to consider that she might have been hoodwinked, but quite another for someone else to think it of her. And I knew how much Martha valued the banker's good opinion. He spoke again. "Does it seem possible to you that those organising the meetings in the vinegar yard could have known that Mr Welford and his wife had a bit of money put aside?"

I thought for a moment. "They could, yes," I confirmed. "They could easily find out that Welford was employed in a reputable premises, with wealthy customers. And Welford did say that he was invited to a special meeting, with only the most important brethren in attendance."

The banker raised an eyebrow. "So perhaps they choose their targets. What about the slaughter man's widow? Could they have discovered that her late husband had left her some savings?"

"Mrs Woodman, yes, probably," I agreed. "Although she was spoken to in the public meeting – not in a special private one, like Welford."

"In other words," said Freame slowly, "they invite different targets to different meetings, depending on how much they have to offer. A clever scheme, as it makes the wealthier victims feel particularly chosen."

"That's the very word that Welford used," I said. "Chosen for his true faith, he said."

"Chosen for his large purse, more likely," said the banker.

CHAPTER SEVENTEEN

A warning in Carnaby Market

TUESDAY 30TH SEPTEMBER 1828

After a profitless morning trying unsuccessfully to run a thief to ground, I turned my step back towards the police office. As I rounded the corner into Great Marlborough Street, I saw Wilson waiting at the foot of the steps, looking first one way and then the other, obviously waiting for someone. He spotted me and started walking quickly to meet me.

"There's a body been found, sir," he said. "Carnaby Market. Throat cut." He made the appropriate gesture across his own neck.

"You don't need me for that these days, lad," I said, thinking – if I am honest – of how nice it would be to sit down for a while in the warmth of the back office, and maybe even slip off my boots for a few minutes.

"No, sir," said Wilson, stepping impatiently from foot to foot, "not in the ordinary run of things. But you should see this one."

I sighed and put all thoughts of the back office out of my mind. Together we walked down Carnaby Street and turned left. Although the market itself had closed a few years earlier and been demolished to make way for the new buildings that we now walked past, everyone still referred to the area as Carnaby Market. Left just far enough off the main street that it would not be spotted immediately was a body, propped up against the wall of the alley, legs out but with a cloth of some sort over the torso and head. Standing watch over it was one of our regular message lads, Jimmy.

"No-one's been near, Mr Plank," he said eagerly as soon as he saw me. "I kept him covered up, just like Mr Wilson told me. Do you want to see him?" Jimmy reached down as though to pull off the cloth, which I could see now was the old horse blanket that Tom Neale kept behind the counter at Great Marlborough Street.

"In a moment, Jimmy," I said. "Did you find him?"

He shook his head. "Not me, no, Mr Plank, sir. It was Mary -" he stopped and went red, "I mean, it was a young lady who prefers not to leave her name. She was meeting a gentleman friend hereabouts, and she saw him. Gave her a real fright. She said that I should tell you – tell the constables. So I went and fetched Mr Wilson, and then I waited here when he went for you, Mr Plank, sir." Jimmy smiled at me eagerly, and I put my hand into my pocket.

"You have done well, Jimmy; you have been a great help." I handed him three coins and then added one more. "If you see Mary again, you might pass that one on to her. Now, off you go: Constable Wilson and I need to work."

Jimmy closed his grubby hand around the coins and ran off into Carnaby Street.

"Well then," I said, "what is it that I really need to see?"

Wilson bent down and pulled the blanket off the body. It was Charlie Gordon, as pale as paper and with his poor arm bent uselessly behind him. Across his throat, as Wilson had said, was a bright red wound.

"There," said Wilson, pointing. Around Charlie's neck was a cardboard label on a piece of string, such as might be put on a package. I crouched and carefully picked up the label, the corner of which was stained with Charlie's blood. I turned it to the light. "Warning," it said. "Too much vinegar can split Planks."

"Capital P," said Wilson softly. "It's talking about you."

Conant read the label again and then looked at me.

"I think Constable Wilson is right," he said. "This is definitely meant for you. The man had his throat cut, you said? Split from ear to ear, as they say?"

"Yes, sir," said Wilson. I looked at him in surprise, as he usually left it to me to answer the magistrate's questions, but he continued. "And I think that Constable Plank was meant to be the one who found the body. Charlie Gordon's a long way from home. I asked Mr Neale about him."

Conant sat at his table and indicated that we should do the same, but this was more than Wilson would contemplate and he took up his usual – and on this occasion protective – position behind my chair.

"So Mr Gordon is not a Piccadilly man?" asked Conant.

"No, sir," I said. "Charlie's territory is – or rather was – Finsbury."

The magistrate raised an eyebrow. "Out past Clerkenwell, then. As Constable Wilson says, a long way from home. And what did Mr Gordon do in Finsbury?"

"When our paths first crossed he was a thief, but in recent years I heard that he'd moved into receiving and fencing," I replied. "Filching is a young man's game: you need to be light-heeled."

"And so we come to your connection with our dead thief," said Conant, and waited.

"Yes," I said, choosing my words carefully. "Last Wednesday I went to a religious gathering near Bunhill Fields. At a vinegar yard – the one Mr Welford told us about. Charlie Gordon was also there, and he recognised me. We spoke a few words, for old times' sake."

"But there was no argument? No disagreement?" asked the magistrate.

"No, sir – it was perfectly cordial," I said smoothly.

Too smoothly, perhaps. Conant gave me a long, appraising look. "Mr Gordon – whatever his line of work these days – did not travel three miles west in order to lie down in an alleyway and cut his own throat. I think Constable Wilson is right: this is a message for you. Someone at that gathering saw you speaking to Mr Gordon, and we need to know who that was and what they fear that you will find. It must be substantial, to go to such trouble – and to rob a man of his life. While Constable Wilson has the unhappy task of telling Mr Gordon's family what has happened, perhaps you should go over the evening again in your mind. Every detail."

I stood. "Yes, sir."

Wilson walked ahead of me to the door, and I could tell from the stern set of his shoulders that he was angry.

Wilson was silent as we walked home, but it was the sort of silence that suggests that there is plenty that will be said. When we drew level with the Crown and Sceptre on the corner of Queen Ann Street, I stopped.

"I'm thirsty," I said. "I am minded to take a nip. And I daresay my purse can stretch to a pint for you."

Wilson looked surprised: we rarely drank while in uniform, but I reasoned that it was preferable to clear the air and put up with Martha's questions about the ale on my breath rather than to have the whole matter of Charlie's bloody warning come out over dinner. But he followed me inside readily enough and found us a small table in a quiet corner while I ordered our drinks. The potboy brought them over and cleared the dead men from our table.

Wilson took a deep draught and observed, "I see you decided on a pint yourself."

"Aye," I said. "It's not every day a man is threatened in such a colourful and gruesome manner." I took a large mouthful and then put my tankard on the table. "I should think Mrs Plank would find it very upsetting to hear about this. She might not realise – as we constables do – that such threats are usually empty. Meant to scare rather than to, well, rather than to happen." Although my words were easy, I must admit that the sight of that ghastly wound had unnerved me. My presence at the meeting in the vinegar yard had obviously interrupted something far more important, far more sinister than the fleecing of a few coins from gullible believers. I took another drink. "And so I think that we should not mention it to her."

Wilson put down his tankard and drew himself up. "You must know by now, sir, the great regard I have for

Mrs Plank," he said with great seriousness. "I would protect her like I would my own mother."

"Thank you, Wilson," I said. "You're a good lad."

He held up a hand to stop me. "And I would protect you too, sir, if you would let me. I'm not a greenhead any longer – I've been working with you for coming up four years now. I know I'm not the quickest study, but I watch and I listen. And I would have gone to the vinegar yard with you." He looked steadily at me. "Why did you go alone, sir? Do you not trust me?" The pain was clear in his voice.

And I realised that he was right: he was a constable of some experience now, and a good one too. He still made the sort of impetuous mistakes that any young man will make until age introduces him to caution and fear, but he did not let them put him off trying again – and much success in life comes from determination and sticking with things. He deserved to know what I suspected. I drained my tankard and looked questioningly at Wilson's before signalling the potboy for two more pints.

CHAPTER EIGHTEEN

Heaven and Hell

TUESDAY 2ND OCTOBER 1828

Wilson and I were readying ourselves to walk home, the thought of Martha's promised rabbit stew on our minds, when there was a quiet knock on the door of the back office and in came Thin Billy, Mr Conant's footman. He rarely ventured out of the domestic parts of the building, and looked uneasy in his surroundings.

"Constable Plank," he said, "Mr Conant wonders if he might trouble you for a few minutes." He glanced at Wilson and then back at me. "A rather delicate matter. Miss Lily is with him."

The magistrate's daughter was a regular sight in her father's rooms. Although they maintained their family residence at Portland Place, with Lily mistress of it since her mother's death some years earlier, Conant himself spent occasional nights living over the shop, as he called it. And when he was from home, a visit from his bright and intelligent daughter would always lighten his mood. Wilson, however, found her presence distracting and unsettling – as indeed would I have done, at his age, for she was a fine-looking girl – and he quickly put on his hat.

"I could wait for you, sir," he said, inching his way towards the door. "Or perhaps I should go on ahead, and warn Mrs Plank that you have been delayed."

"You go on, lad," I said. "But mind that I shall expect my full share of that stew when I get home."

Thin Billy led me up the stairs to the magistrate's rooms. At the door he stopped before knocking, and turned to me.

"Miss Lily's crying," he whispered. "Very distressed. And whatever it is, he thinks you can help." He tapped softly on the door and then stepped back to let me go in, closing the door gently behind me.

Lily Conant was sitting in her father's armchair by the fire, while Conant himself was crouched beside her on the footstool. He looked up at me and scrambled to his feet.

"Well now, Lily, my dear," he said in tones of forced jollity, "here is Constable Plank come to see us." He beckoned me over. "Dry your eyes, now, there's a good girl."

He patted his pockets and I wordlessly took out my handkerchief and handed it to him. He bent down to pass it to his daughter.

"Really, papa?" she said, sniffing. "A third handkerchief? Yours, mine and now Constable Plank's?"

I smiled at her. "In that case, Miss Conant, I shall retrieve mine – Mrs Plank certainly has no need of more laundry."

The young lady smiled in return – not a full smile, to be sure, but enough to reassure her papa, who, like many men, regarded feminine tears with a combination of bafflement and fear. I like to think that I am more robust, having seen perhaps rather more crying women than most, and I have learned that in many cases tears can be cleansing. It is silent despair that I dread.

"Perhaps Miss Conant might like a small glass of madeira," I suggested.

"Excellent idea," said Conant, walking over to the decanters and plainly grateful to have something practical to do. "Although I think I shall add a splash of water – it can be quite strong."

I looked down at Miss Lily and she smiled conspiratorially. Although she was a grown woman of twenty-two years, it was plain to all except Conant himself that he still saw her as a beloved child.

"And a glass of something for you, Sam?" asked the magistrate, bringing over a delicate glass to his daughter.

I shook my head. "A coffee, perhaps, sir, thank you, if Thin Billy has filled the pot recently." I brought over a pair of dining chairs and placed them near the armchair, where Miss Lily had curled her legs up under her and was now sipping her drink. Her eyes were still a little red and swollen, but we were over the worst.

Conant brought over my coffee and a glass of port for himself, and we sat in the dining chairs. After a few moments, the magistrate reached up to put his glass on the mantelpiece and looked at his daughter. "I think you should tell Constable Plank what you have told me, my dear. He has seen something similar recently, and he may be able to help." He held out his hand and Lily gave him her glass.

"Constable Plank," she said, "do you believe in Heaven?"

I raised my eyebrows. "Heaven?" I asked. She nodded. "You mean where God resides?"

"More as a place to go after death," she replied.

I thought and then spoke slowly, choosing my words – not for her benefit, but for my own. It was an important question. "I am a practical man, Miss Lily. I spend my days – as indeed does your father – thinking about and seeing the very worst that people can do." I paused. This was not a confession to make lightly, even to oneself.

Miss Conant leaned forward and touched my hand. "Please tell me. I want to know."

"In that case, no, I do not believe in Heaven, or indeed in Hell," I said. "I think they are images made up to serve a cause. I think our reward and our punishment both come on Earth. If we live a good life, a useful life, we are remembered with fondness and regard – and that is what we call Heaven. If we live a wicked life of selfishness, we are cursed by those who come after and their recriminations consign us to what we call Hell."

Miss Conant nodded. "But it does not always work like that, does it? Sometimes good people suffer and wicked people flourish." She smiled sadly. "But I am not trying to tie you up in philosophical knots, constable. I have a particular reason for asking." She leaned back in her chair. "Yesterday evening I heard a woman claim that she can speak to those who are in Heaven." The magistrate and I looked at each other, and – catching this glance – Lily frowned slightly. "She was very credible. Very convincing. And she knew things that previously had been known only to the person who had died and those left behind."

"What sort of things, Miss Lily?" I asked, taking out my notebook. "May I?" I asked.

She nodded. "I have a friend called Catherine Palgrave. Her mother died last year, after falling down the stairs."

"It was a very sad story," added her father. "Two or three little ones left behind, if I remember correctly."

"Yes," said Miss Conant. "Catherine is the eldest, but two of her brothers and a sister are not yet ten years of age."

"And the father is a Naval man, I believe – a captain?" The magistrate looked pleased with his powers of recall.

"Just so, papa – and it is Captain Palgrave who is at the heart of it." Miss Conant looked across at her father. "Captain Palgrave is a brute, papa. He has a temper – a violent temper. Catherine has learned to keep out of his way when he is in one of his rages."

Conant's face was pale. "Have you seen him in a rage, Lily? Has he…?" He could not finish his question.

His daughter shook her head. "No; I understand he is careful to confine his outbursts to the family. But I called on Catherine one day and found her weeping, and she told me everything. She longs to marry and leave her father's household, but the only men she meets are the Naval officers he brings home, and she fears them all, assuming them to be out of his mould. She cannot believe that there are gentle men in the world – men like you, papa, and like Constable Plank." She smiled at me. A memory came to me of how Martha had flinched from my touch when we first met, accustomed as she was to the drunken furies of her own father.

"But what has this to do with your enquiry about Heaven?" I asked, to distract the magistrate from whatever imaginings were torturing him.

"Ah yes," said Miss Conant. "This woman told Catherine that she had spoken to her late mother who wanted to pass on a message. We all thought it would be words of comfort, about Mrs Palgrave being at peace and wishing her daughter well." She looked at me and I nodded. "But instead she said the most awful things. She said that Mrs Palgrave had not fallen down the stairs. She said that her husband had beaten her so severely that she had died, and he had put the body at the foot of the stairs to make it look like an accident." Miss Lily clasped her hands. "How could anyone have known that? Catherine was upset, of course, but not surprised – I think she always feared that it would happen – but no-one outside the family knew what he was like. What he is like."

"But you did, Miss Lily," I said, looking up from my notebook. "And if you did, then others probably did as well."

"Indeed," said the magistrate. "Captain Palgrave's valet, for instance – he cannot be unaware of the man's temper. And if one servant knows, then it is likely that they all do."

"And it takes only a few coins placed in the right hands to buy useful information," I said. "Was this a public gathering, where you and Miss Palgrave heard the woman speak?"

Miss Lily shook her head. "No, it was a private evening at Catherine's house. Her maid told her that she had heard this woman at a public event – a herald, she called her – and that perhaps Catherine would be comforted to hear from her mother."

The magistrate and I exchanged glances, but once again Miss Lily was too quick for us.

"You think that the maid was involved?" she asked. "That she invited the woman in, and told her what to say?"

"It could be," I said. "I have been to a similar gathering myself, and although it seems plausible, the messages that are shared may not be as secret as they seem."

"But why would this woman want to distress Catherine?" asked Miss Conant.

Her father leaned over and patted her on the hand. "That is not the aim, my dear – not at all. It is an unfortunate consequence, that is all. Her aim is simply to make money. And to do that she has to convince you that she has a genuine skill. I take it that you young ladies contributed a little something?"

His daughter nodded. "We did, yes. But not just for her, papa – she is about to have a baby and will not be able to hold meetings for some months."

By the time I reached home, Wilson had gone. Martha went to the stove and ladled out the rather meagre portion of stew that he had seen fit to leave me.

"I did put in another couple of potatoes," she said, "but there's no more rabbit." Once we would have laughed about Wilson's endless appetite, but there had been precious little laughter in our house recently. Martha sat for a moment, watching me eat, but then stood again and busied herself clearing pots. I ate in silence, and when she heard me put down my spoon she took my bowl and put a slice of plum cake in front of me. "William polished off the walnut loaf, but I hid this from him," she said. I looked at her, and there was the very tiniest hint of a smile.

"Sit down with me, Mar," I said. "Please."

She looked around the kitchen and then shrugged and sat – but only half on her chair, as though poised for flight. She leaned on the table but then thought better of it and put her hands in her lap, perhaps sensing that I might reach for them.

"Last Wednesday I saw you at the meeting in the vinegar yard," I said.

Martha's look darkened. "Are you following me, Sam?" she asked with quiet anger. "Can you not stand the thought of me having something of my own, but that you have to interfere?"

It had not occurred to me that she would think this. "It was coincidence, my love – I swear," I said.

"Coincidence?" she said. "Do not take me for a fool, Samuel. What on earth would take you to the vinegar yard, if not in pursuit of me?"

"A man was murdered today," I said.

"If you think that changing the subject…" she started.

"I am not changing the subject," I protested. "You asked what took me to the vinegar yard and I am telling you." Martha glared at me but said nothing. "His name was Charlie Gordon, and we had known each other for years. He was a rogue through and through, but not a violent one. I last saw him alive at the vinegar yard that evening."

"Was it this Mr Gordon that you were following, then?" she asked.

I shook my head. "I was trying to understand what made a man kill his wife. You remember Mr Welford – smothered his wife in her bed, back in the summer."

Martha frowned. "Mr Welford? But I thought you said he was mad. What has he to do with our meetings?"

There was nothing for it but to tell her everything. Martha listened. When I had finished, she sat back and folded her arms.

"I know what you are thinking, Samuel Plank," she said.

"Do you?" I asked.

She stood up and put her hands on the table, leaning towards me. "You are thinking that I am a silly creature."

I started to speak but she held up her hand. "You are thinking that Alice and I have fallen for some sort of trickery. I do not deny that it sounds as though Alice has taken money that she should not, but then grief takes people in strange ways. Yes, perhaps she has given this money to Eliza. But that woman has a gift, Sam – a gift. She sees and hears things that we do not." She pointed at me. "Don't you dare raise an eyebrow at me – don't you dare," she all but hissed. "You think yourself so very clever, discussing it all with Mr Conant and passing judgement." I was thankful that I had omitted to tell her of my visit to Freame. "But just because you cannot explain something, it does not mean that it is not possible. And what the heralds do is possible, Sam. I should know, because I have had a message. Not as special as Alice's message, to be sure, but still. And for the comfort Alice has gained from Eliza's promise of a new baby to come one day, well, I think it is money more than well spent. Make sure you put your dish on the side when you've finished."

And with that, my wife stalked out of the kitchen and I could hear her angry footsteps going up the stairs.

I did as I was told and cleared away my dish and my cup. I checked that the front and back doors were secure, that the lanterns were trimmed and that the shutters were tight against the night. I took my time over all of these tasks. Growing up with a drunken father who was violent when in his cups, Martha both loathed and feared shows of temper. She had once confessed that she dreaded discovering the same ill humour in herself and so she took particular care to nurture a slowness to anger – indeed, it was one of the many things that drew me to her. But, as is often the case with those who rarely rise to rage, when it happens, it is explosive, and then mercifully quick to subside. The longer I took to join her upstairs, the quieter I was likely to find her.

Martha was in bed, curled tightly on her side. I quietly shed my clothes and shivered into my nightshirt before climbing in next to her.

"Mar?" I asked softly. "Talk to me, Mar."

I waited for a few moments, hardly daring to breathe, and then she turned over and put her head on my shoulder. Under the bedding, I took hold of her hands and held them in mine. I waited.

"Alice went to two meetings on her own," she said eventually. "She told me about them, and about the message she had received about a baby boy. I was like you, Sam – I didn't think it was true. Well, I knew that Alice believed it, but I thought it was a trick of some sort. But I didn't want to mock her, or make her sad again – it was the first time she had seemed happy about anything since... well, since then." I squeezed her hands but said nothing. "So I asked to go along with her, to see what they were up to for myself. So she took me, and I met Mr Buxton. And I liked him. He was kind and genuine – a good man. A bit like you, I thought. And that very first evening, the herald spoke to me."

"Eliza?" I asked.

Martha nodded against my chest. "She said that my mother wanted to tell me something. My mother, Sam."

Martha moved her head to look up at me. Her mother had died long before I met Martha, when Martha was still a girl – perhaps thirty-five years ago. She had left behind a brood of children, Martha the eldest at only eight, in the care of a man who spent more time drunk than sober, and was unpleasant company in either state. Martha's memories of her mother were precious and fond, and I know that there had been many times – at our betrothal, during the early turbulent years of our marriage, and with each baby that came to nought – when she had sorely missed any maternal counsel or comfort.

"And what did your mother say to you, my dear?" I asked gently.

"She said she was proud to see the fine woman I have become, and the good choice I had made in my husband. She knew that you were a constable, and said it was a good, steady job for a respectable man." She paused for a few seconds. "She said she knew the disappointments we have had, and that we are childless. And she said that I was to stop minding, and to stop wishing. That I should take comfort instead from all the people I love and who love me, and who need me. She mentioned Alice by name, Sam, and she knew about the school."

As I listened, I thought back to my conversation with Tom Neale. If it was simply clever use of knowledge, as with the slaughter man's widow, how could Buxton and Eliza have found out all this about my wife – and about me? Only one possibility came to me: Alice.

But for the moment, more important than any of that was the woman lying beside me, and what I should say to her.

"And what do you think of her advice, my dear?" I asked her, reaching up to stroke her cheek.

"I think it wise," said Martha. "Hard to take, but wise – like all the best advice." She put up her hand and stroked my face in turn. "I think perhaps it is time to accept what God has chosen for me, and to be thankful for what he has sent."

"In that case," I said, "I am grateful for the herald's message."

"So am I," said Martha sleepily. "Perhaps you should come with me next time, Sam. There may be a message for you, from your father."

CHAPTER NINETEEN

Good behaviour for life

MONDAY 6TH OCTOBER 1828

I am a man accustomed to my own company. It sounds odd to say that, as I live in the most crowded city in the world, with never a moment when all is still, but everyone knows that the place where it is impossible to be alone is the smallest village. In this great city, with its hundreds of thousands of busy souls, I can keep to myself as much as I choose. But sometimes my mind worries at a subject for too long, teasing and shaking it to no good effect, and that is when I find my step turning eastwards towards Newgate, as it did a few days after Martha had told me about her message from her mother.

After exchanging the usual pleasantries – or what passes for pleasantries in their grizzled fraternity – with the turnkeys on the prison gate, I walked across the courtyard to John Wontner's office. Most visitors to the prison were accompanied, but I was now so well-known to everyone – both in my professional capacity and as a friend of the keeper – that they were happy to let me make my own way. I knocked on the door and, receiving no reply, let myself in. I was just pouring myself a tumbler of barley water from the jug on the desk when Wontner himself returned.

"A toast," he said warmly, shaking my hand. "Pour me one too, Sam, and we'll wet the baby's head." I raised an eyebrow. "A boy – a bonny one, with a shock of black hair and strong lungs. Mother thriving too, but then Sally Gregson's an old hand at this – it's her seventh, and the fifth born in here." He swigged down his drink and poured another. "I don't think there's much on the outside for her. Larceny."

I nodded. If a thief stole something of little value with no aggravating circumstances – no violence, or house-breaking, for instance – the charge would be larceny rather than theft or shoplifting, and the sentence a few months in Newgate. And there were plenty like Sally for whom a mattress in a prison cell was a sight better than whatever midden they called home.

Wontner and I both sat down. "You must have been on my mind, Sam," he said, casting his eye over his desk to check for new paperwork.

"Aye?" I said.

"Sally was talking about a name for the new one, and she's already used John for number three – or was it number four?" He looked at me and winked. "So I suggested Samuel, and she was very taken with it. Let's hope the little chap takes after his namesake and not his mother when it comes to morals." He sat back in his chair. "Nothing urgent, so I am at your disposal."

"Have you ever spoken to the dead, John?" I asked.

If the keeper was surprised by my question he did not show it and simply looked at me levelly. "I have," he said, "on many occasions."

"And have they ever replied?" I asked.

"Never once," he confirmed.

"Then we have had the same experience," I said, "but it seems that there are those who would like to convince us otherwise." I described what I had seen at the gathering in the vinegar yard, and then told him what Miss Conant had witnessed at the home of her friend.

"And you think that both meetings were organised by the same person, with the same woman used at both?" he asked.

"I cannot be sure; after all, there are plenty of young women with child in London," I replied. "But it seems likely – too much of a coincidence."

"I agree," he said. "Do you have any idea who could be behind these deceptions?"

I nodded. "My initial thought was Buxton – the preacher at the vinegar yard. But then the warning I received, naming me specifically, when he did not know me..." I saw the look of concern on the keeper's face. "Ah yes, there is something I neglected to tell you."

Wontner listened as I described the grisly finding in the alleyway. When I had finished he shook his head. "There will be few to mourn Mr Gordon, I fear." Then he stopped. "Buxton, you said? The man at the vinegar yard?"

I nodded. "John Buxton, yes."

"Handsome-looking fellow?" asked Wontner. "Broad – like a farmer?" He held out his hands to indicate width. "Not from London?"

"Indeed," I said. "That's the one."

"Then you're in luck, Sam. I had him here once." The keeper stood and went to his bookcase where, in a system known only to himself, he kept the files relating to his prisoners. After a couple of minutes he turned around triumphantly. "John Buxton – religious offences – three years," he read from the front of the folder, and then handed it to me. "You can read it here, if you wish. I have an errand to run and will be back in a few minutes."

I opened the folder and started to read. John Buxton had been indicted on a charge of publishing a wicked and blasphemous libel of the holy scriptures, and his trial had taken place some six years earlier, in July of 1822. Giving evidence against him was William Miller, a Bow Street runner – although of course Miller referred to himself as a patrolman, as did all his fellows, considering the description 'runner' something of an insult. Miller told the court that he had visited a shop in Fleet Street, Carlile's at number 84, and asked the man serving there – whom he identified in court as the prisoner Buxton – whether he had Palmer's "Principles of Nature" for sale. Buxton had said that he did, and named the price as a sovereign. Miller had baulked at the cost, saying that he had heard that the price was two shillings, and that the person commissioning the purchase – his master in the country – would be disappointed. Buxton had asked which part of the country, and the runner had said Lincolnshire. Buxton said that he knew it well, having come from Spalding only a few days earlier himself, and so would let him have the book for two shillings. The records in the folder noted that Miller had submitted to the court the book in question, which he had marked 'Bought at Carlile's shop, 31st May 1822, William Miller'.

Buxton was then quizzed about his religious beliefs. When asked what he considered to be a binding obligation, he replied, "Swearing on the Gospels". And when asked what he considered to be blasphemy, he replied, "Any attempt to vilify the Christian religion, promulgated by our Saviour and his Apostles". He then apparently read a long defence – which no-one had cared to preserve for the records – contending that his prosecution was inconsistent with Christian values. He was found guilty, sentenced to three years' imprisonment in Newgate, and ordered to enter into his own recognisance one hundred pounds for good behaviour for life.

Just as I finished reading, Wontner returned. I handed him the file.

"I take it there has been no call on the hundred pounds?" I asked.

The keeper shook his head. "Not as far as I know. He served his time here quietly enough; indeed, I seem to recall that he was quite helpful, helping some of the lads to master their letters. If he had come to the notice of the court again, for a second serious offence, word would have reached me. There are plenty still here who remember him." He put the folder back into the bookcase and took his seat again.

"Perhaps he learned more from them than they did from him," I said. "Perhaps he came here a well-meaning Christian, and left three years later a swindler. And now he takes advantage of the grieving and the desperate, fooling them into believing that he can comfort them."

Wontner raised an eyebrow at me. "It is not like you, Sam, to think the worst of someone."

"Ah well," I said. "You might not think so well of him if he had snared your wife in his deceit."

"Martha?" asked Wontner in astonishment. "What on earth do you mean?"

As objectively as I could – although it was hard to keep my anger in check – I repeated to the keeper what Martha had told me. I also shared with him my suspicion that the information apparently known by the herald had come not from Martha's dead mother, but from Alice.

"That sounds very likely," agreed Wontner. "Alice had been going to the meetings for a while before Martha joined her, and might well have talked to other people about her dear friend." He shook his head sadly. "I am sorry to hear of this, Sam – for both you and Martha."

"The difficulty for me," I said, and as I spoke I realised that this was indeed what had been troubling me, "is that as Sam Plank the husband, I am truly grateful to the herald. Her message, with its recommendation of acceptance and its reminder that Martha, although not a mother, is valued by so many, has brought my wife a peace that she has lacked for many weeks. Perhaps years." Wontner nodded in sympathy. "But as a constable," I continued, "I cannot tolerate this deception, this fraudulent behaviour which seeks to take advantage of the vulnerable and steal from them. Yes, theft it is. And perhaps worse." I leaned forward. "Tell me, John: do you think Buxton capable of murdering Charlie Gordon – or of ordering his murder? You have spoken to the man; I have seen him only from a distance, and then during a, well, a performance."

Wontner thought for a few moments and then shook his head. "I do not, no. John Buxton was a religious zealot, to be sure, but he used words to convince – not his fists, and certainly not a knife."

"Did he believe in communicating with the dead?" I asked.

"It was not something we discussed, Sam," said the keeper with a smile. "But I can imagine that a man who believes so fervently in life after death might convince himself that such a thing was possible. Or others might convince him."

"Others?" I repeated.

Wontner leaned forward. "We know good and evil, Sam, you and I. And we also know that it is a rare leopard that changes his spots. If a man is essentially good, he may in extremis commit some foul deed, but he will remain at heart a good man."

I thought of Josiah Welford; he was a murderer, of that there was no doubt, but I would not call him evil.

"The John Buxton I knew," continued the keeper, "was a good man. His beliefs may not chime with ours, but I know that they were sincerely held – and not adopted for profit. And – albeit six years later – I imagine that he is still a good man."

"And so you think I must look elsewhere for Charlie's murderer?" I asked.

"I do, Sam – and quickly," said Wontner, nodding. "Whoever he is, he has already shown his ruthless side when threatened. What might he do if he fears that Buxton has outlived his usefulness? Or if he discovers that you have not heeded his warning?"

CHAPTER TWENTY

Alice is from home

WEDNESDAY 8TH OCTOBER 1828 – MORNING

It was now my turn to be quiet at home. I could feel Martha looking at me as I ate my breakfast, and when she passed behind my chair she put a hand on my shoulder, but she said nothing. In truth, I was relieved that she did not press me. How could I tell her that I so mistrusted the very thing that seemed to bring her comfort? It would make her feel foolish, as though I was questioning her judgement. But I had forgotten how lonely it was to bear a trouble alone, and that realisation served only to sour my mood even further.

I put on my coat and – as was her habit – Martha walked around behind me to check that I was presentable. When she reappeared in front of me I leaned forward to kiss her cheek and she grasped my hand.

"Come home to me tonight, Sam," she said fiercely. "Come home."

Like many men, I am rather cowardly when it comes to examining my own feelings, and so I was glad when I left the house and saw Wilson waiting for me at the corner. When he had not knocked on the door at his usual time I had assumed that I would see him at Great Marlborough Street instead – and that would entail a walk alone with my troubling thoughts.

"Running late?" I said as I drew level with him.

"I've been here for ten minutes," he replied with a note of injury in his voice.

"Then you should have come to the house," I continued. "Mrs Plank is always pleased to see you."

But as I said it, I knew that the welcome Wilson used to find at Martha's table was much less ready these days. Martha's sadness and grief coloured everything she touched, and I did not blame him for keeping his distance. We turned into Great Titchfield Street and both lowered our heads against the cold autumn wind that came whistling towards us.

"That's what my mother calls a lazy wind," said Wilson, hunching his shoulders. "It goes through you instead of around you." We walked on in silence for a couple of minutes. As we drew level with Oxford Market, Wilson stopped. He seemed uncertain and then walked towards the market building, beckoning me to follow him until we were standing in the lee of the building, under the porch, sheltered from the worst of the wind.

"I didn't dare come to the house this morning because Mrs Plank can always tell when I am worried," he said. "And she asks such clever questions that, before I know where I am, I have told her everything."

I almost laughed, so similar was his experience to my own. Martha is a rare one for sniffing out the truth. But I contented myself with asking, "And what is it that you did not want her to know? Or are you too embarrassed even to tell me?"

Wilson looked at me, frowning. "It was not for my sake that I did not want to tell her, sir," he said. "It was to spare her, after, well, after all that has happened in recent weeks." He swallowed hard and looked away for a moment.

"It has been hard on all of us, lad," I said. He nodded, his face still turned from me. I looked about me at the stallholders setting up for the day; I knew that Wilson would tell me what was troubling him once he had found the words.

He turned to look at me, misery clear on his face. I did not need Martha's skills to know that something was dreadfully wrong.

"It's Alice," he said. "She's gone missing."

"When did anyone last see her?" asked Martha. Despite Wilson's protestations, I had abandoned all thoughts of the police office and returned home with him in tow. Martha had been in the yard, shaking out a rug, but as soon as she saw us and our stricken faces she put aside her chores and led us indoors. Wilson hung back, looking daggers at me, but I ignored his finer feelings and told him to sit. Martha sat between us, looking from one to the other as we told our tale.

"Were you the last to see her, William?" she asked when her first question went unanswered.

Wilson shook his head. "I saw her on Sunday afternoon," he said. "I've taken to calling at the Blue Boar. I did it when little Martha... was there. And it would have been unkind to stop, now that Alice needs me." He flushed. "Now that she needs all of us."

Martha patted his hand briskly. "You are right, William – she does need you. So you saw her as usual this Sunday afternoon." He nodded. "And today is Wednesday. How do you know that she is missing? Did you call in again?"

Wilson dug into his coat pocket and pulled out a scrap of paper. He handed it to me. It was a handbill advertising an entertainment of some sort at a theatre, but on the back was a handwritten message. I turned it to the light and read aloud. "Dear Mr Wilson, Have you seen Alice?

She is from home since Sunday evening. Pray send word that she is, God willing, safe with you or with Mrs Plank. Yours, George Atkins." I looked at Wilson.

"It was delivered to me this morning," he said. "She has not come to me, and not to you either," we both shook our heads, "so where is she? You don't think she's gone back to… to what she did before, do you?"

This time Martha did not pat Wilson's hand: instead, she clasped it in both of hers. "You listen to me, William Wilson," she said sternly. "People took advantage of Alice in the past, and she did what she had to do to survive. But she is a long way from that now. She has a home and respectable work and people who care for her. She will not return to her old world, I feel sure – because she has tasted a much better world, full of love. Now we must put our heads together to try to think where she could have gone, so that we can find her and remind her how loved she is."

"I have an idea where we might find her," I said. Martha and Wilson both looked at me. "The vinegar yard, if there is a meeting there this evening."

"It's Wednesday," said Martha, "so yes. Starting at seven o'clock, although Mr Buxton and the herald will be there perhaps an hour earlier."

"Seven o'clock!" said Wilson. "But that's ten hours away – anything might happen to her in that time. We must look for her now." He got to his feet.

"But where, lad?" I asked. "She could be anywhere. She's like a wounded animal, hiding away. But she feels safe and comforted at the vinegar yard, and I'm fairly sure she'll make her way there this evening. And you and I will be waiting for her."

"I'll come with you," said Martha.

I shook my head. "No, my dear."

"But why on earth not?" she asked.

Wilson looked down at his hands as he stood awkwardly by the door.

I chose my words carefully. "It may be that the organisers of these meetings are not entirely honest." I looked at Martha but she said nothing. I continued. "Should matters eventually be brought before the magistrates, I do not want you to be involved. This evening I need to protect Alice, and I cannot do that if I am concerned about you. Please, Martha. Promise me that you will not come."

Martha was silent for a long moment. "If I must, Sam, then I will promise. But you are wrong about our meetings, and it is unkind of you to ask it."

CHAPTER TWENTY-ONE

George

WEDNESDAY 8TH OCTOBER 1828 – EVENING

After an uncomfortable day during which we tried to distract ourselves with other tasks, Wilson and I set off eastwards. As we walked I told him the bare bones of the message that the herald had delivered to Martha. Quite correctly, he expressed no sympathy or opinion, but simply made a note in his book. Part way along the City Road we stopped for refreshment, as I thought it very unlikely that I would find any supper kept for me later that evening. We were both in plain coats, and as we approached the wooden gate of the vinegar yard I pointed to the crumbs down Wilson's front – all that remained of the large pie that he had just eaten. He smiled like a naughty boy and brushed himself down with both hands.

We waited until a small group of people filed into the yard through the small gate and then joined them, following them into the large room filled with benches. Wilson is much more conspicuous than I am, with his height, and I quickly led him to a bench near the back of the room and indicated that he should sit. A man and woman alongside us nodded in greeting. As on the previous occasion, a crate was placed at the front of the room, and indeed a young woman was waiting on a seat against the wall. But it was not Eliza – perhaps there was a whole circus of them trained in tricks and illusion.

Just then Wilson nudged me and jerked his head towards the door. It was Alice. She stopped and looked around, and Wilson and I quickly turned our heads from her.

"Thank God she is safe," breathed Wilson.

"Indeed," I whispered in reply.

When we dared to look again, she was taking a seat at a bench in the middle of the room, her back to us. As she sat, she carefully unwound her shawl, which had been coiled tightly around her against the chill night air. The woman next to her, a grandmotherly type, leaned towards her and smiled. They both gazed down at whatever was in Alice's arms and then Alice shifted her position and adjusted her burden. Looking over her shoulder, seemingly directly at us, was a tiny baby.

I turned to Wilson, and from the shock on his face I could see that he was as confused as I was. Not wishing to sit through another pantomime of speaking to the dead, I indicated to Wilson that he should wait outside while I made my way between the benches, now crowded with people, to where Alice was sitting with the baby. I touched her gently on the shoulder and she looked up at me and smiled in recognition and welcome.

"Mr Plank," she said. "How strange that you should be here too. Is Mrs Plank with you?"

"She is not, no, my dear," I said, "but William is outside. We have all been concerned about you. Come home with me, and Mrs Plank will be so pleased to see you. To see you both." I held out my arms for the baby, and Alice handed it to me without hesitation. She gathered her shawl about her, said a quiet farewell to the old woman beside her, and followed me to the door. Here she paused and looked back into the room.

"I shall miss Mr Buxton's service, but then I have already been blessed," she said. She kissed her fingers and touched them to the baby's head.

Wilson was waiting outside the main gate to the yard, a coach ready beside him. "I thought you might..." he started, nodding towards the vehicle.

"Quite right," I said. "Now let Wilson help you up into the coach, Alice, and then I will hand you the baby."

"George," she said, stepping up. "His name is George, after Mr Atkins. Him and his wife, they have been so kind. You are all so kind."

As the coach rattled through the evening streets, Alice rarely looked out but instead was preoccupied with the child, leaning over him and murmuring little nonsenses as mothers do. And Wilson and I could not think of a single thing to say.

"Well," said Martha, sitting heavily into her chair. "They are both sound asleep." I handed her a cup of tea and she drank almost all of it before putting it onto the table beside her and shaking her head. Wilson and I had passed the time peaceably enough, with me reading aloud pieces from the evening newspaper, but neither of us had thought of much but the drama playing itself out in the tiny room overhead.

Wilson shifted on the hard chair he had carried in from the kitchen. "What do you think, Mrs Plank? Did she tell you what has happened?" he asked.

"She did, William, yes. Well, that is to say that she told me the story from her side of things – you and Sam will have to fill in the rest, I fear." Martha sighed. "As I am sure Sam has told you, Alice and I have been attending meetings together. There are the Sunday ones at Cooper's Gardens, and then the evening ones at the vinegar yard." Wilson nodded. "At one meeting – before I started accompanying her – Alice was told that little Martha had a message for her." At this point Martha looked fiercely at me and then at Wilson. "I know only too well what Sam thinks of such things, that it is all nonsense, and if you share his view, you can save your breath." Wilson duly saved his breath. Martha went on. "Of course Alice told me what little Martha had said – she was so excited. Little Martha said that she was happy in Heaven, and that she was sending Alice another baby to make her smile again." Martha looked down at her hands. "And I was pleased for her. I assumed it meant that she would one day – perhaps quite soon," here Martha glanced at Wilson, "marry and start another family. She's a young, healthy woman, and another baby would almost certainly come along." Martha stopped and took a deep breath. "But that was not the plan. At the end of that meeting, the herald – Eliza – sought out Alice and spoke to her. Eliza was herself expecting a baby, and she said that Alice might like to touch her belly, for luck. They talked for a while, and then Eliza said that she thought Alice could be her saviour." Martha closed her eyes for a moment before continuing. "Eliza said that she could not keep her baby and that she believed little Martha was telling her to give the child to Alice. All that Alice would need to do was pay for a few bits and pieces for the mother-to-be, and then for the handywoman and her remedies, and a fee to register the birth."

I looked at Wilson. "The two pounds," I said, and he nodded.

"What two pounds?" asked Martha.

"No matter," I said. "I'll explain later. What happened after that?"

"At the next two meetings," said Martha, "Eliza would seek out Alice and talk to her about the baby – to let her feel it kicking, and of course to collect some more money."

"Did you not suspect anything?" I asked.

"Eliza made sure to do this out of my sight, and she told Alice that it had to be their little secret," said Martha sadly. "I think Alice felt that she had to do as she was told, or risk losing the baby. And when the baby was born – a little boy – word was sent to her. She was told to wait two weeks and then come to collect him. That was on Sunday. When she went missing."

"Why didn't she just take him back to the Blue Boar?" I asked. "She obviously sees no wrong in what has happened."

Martha sighed. "She feels guilty. She said that she is so happy with George that she did not feel right about flaunting her happiness in the face of Mr and Mrs Atkins, still mourning their little girl."

"Is she not still mourning little Martha?" I asked.

"Eliza has convinced her that little Martha is safe and happy in heaven, and that she has sent George in her place." Martha shook her head. "Alice's poor mind would rather believe that than dwell on the truth. It is as though she has shut it out."

And as she said it, I realised what had happened to Martha herself.

CHAPTER TWENTY-TWO

The salvation of sinners

WEDNESDAY 15TH OCTOBER 1828 – MORNING

"Bread and corned beef," said Martha as she indicated the covered plate. "I'll be out when you come home this evening, but I don't want you using that as an excuse for stopping at the George and Dragon and filling your belly with ale."

"Out at the vinegar yard?" I asked.

"Of course," said Martha, bustling around the kitchen. "It's Wednesday."

"Is Alice going with you?" I asked.

My wife shook her head. "Not this evening. Now that she's back at the Blue Boar, what with George and the other little ones to look after, she's too tired at the end of the day. Thomas is still a bit weak, and Louisa watches them all so carefully…" She was lost for a moment in her thoughts and then seemed to recollect herself. "Now, it's best grade beef, mind, and not cheap, so make sure you enjoy it."

I'm fond of corned beef – the best grade, as Martha knew, and not the cargo beef made of neck and shank – and I lifted the cloth to take a look. The meat was wrapped in a handbill and some of the words on it caught my eye.

"Where did you get this?" I asked, pointing at the paper.

Martha looked over at it. "I can't remember exactly. I think I was given it at Cooper's Gardens. Yes, that would be it: it was in the bottom of my basket when I went to the butcher. Oh, what are you doing now, Sam? If you leave it unwrapped it will dry out, you know that. Pass it here and I'll find something else."

I carefully folded the handbill and slipped it into my pocket.

"Mrs Plank said that she was given this at Cooper's Gardens?" asked Wilson.

I nodded. We were both looking at the handbill which I had straightened out and laid on the table in the back office of Great Marlborough Street. The printing was, as always with these things, crude and patchy, but the message was clear enough. At the top of the sheet was a drawing of a trio of people, their hands clasped in prayer, looking skywards – for indeed they were out of doors and not in a church, as suggested by the simple trees which served as a background. Below them, in large capital letters, was the exhortation to "Join us in prayer". Then came a paragraph, in slightly smaller but still generous print size, outlining the benefits of doing so: "Unite with your brethren at our gatherings and we shall pray together for the PROMOTION OF HOLINESS among God's people and for the SALVATION OF SINNERS. All are welcome – we shall be glad to see YOU. Kindly invite your neighbours." At the foot of the handbill was a list of the dates and locations of the next meetings.

I pointed to the lower part of the handbill. "This part can be altered, I should think," I said. "The top bit will be standard – the same all over the country – with the details at the bottom adjusted to suit the location. And it is the final sentence that interests me."

Wilson looked again. "A collection shall be made for the needy and the destitute," he read aloud. "Why is that interesting?" he asked.

"When I went to Cooper's Gardens with Mrs Plank," I said, "I noticed that there was no collection, no passing of the plate. It was the same at the vinegar yard, if you remember. I raised the matter with Mr Freame, my Quaker friend, who confirmed that they observe the same practice. They believe that it is the responsibility of each person to give what they can within their community, rather than salve their conscience by dropping a few coins onto the plate each Sunday."

"I can see the sense in that," agreed Wilson.

"So just who is collecting this money, if not the preacher?" I asked. "And where is it going? I am fairly sure that the needy and the destitute will see very little of it. I think it's high time we had a word with John Buxton about his meetings, and as it's Wednesday, I know just where to find him."

CHAPTER TWENTY-THREE

A matter of perspective

WEDNESDAY 15TH OCTOBER 1828 – AFTERNOON

Wilson and I set off for the vinegar yard in the early afternoon. I had in mind to speak to Buxton and be long gone before there was any chance of Martha arriving. Once we were outside the gates of the yard, I stopped and laid a hand on Wilson's arm.

"Now, are you certain that you have yourself under control?" I asked. On the way we had discussed again what we already knew and what we hoped to find out, and whenever Alice was mentioned I could feel Wilson's anger. "I understand that you are upset that Alice has been deceived," I continued when he did not reply, "and that you fear, as I do, what might happen if George is taken from her. But a constable has to be able to put aside his personal desires in order to do the job right and to do the job properly."

"I know," he said gruffly.

"If you don't feel that you can be Constable Wilson rather than William Wilson, you must wait out here for me. I will not think any the less of you – but I will if you come in and then step out of line." We heard the gate being opened. "Remember: Alice is not the only one we need to worry about. If we can put a stop to this, we will protect many more people." I knew that we were both thinking of Martha.

Wilson drew himself up and nodded. "I'm ready," he said, and we stepped through into the yard as the gate was held open for us by a workman and then pulled closed behind us.

John Buxton was alone. He was sitting reading at one of the benches near the front of the room and stood when we walked in.

"Good evening, gentlemen," he called. "You are welcome – early, but welcome." He threaded his way between the tables towards us, his hand out. He was as I remembered him: about as broad as Wilson, although not as tall, and with a friendly, open face and the weathered complexion of a man who spends his days out of doors in the fields. "I have seen you here before, have I not?" he asked as we shook hands.

"You have a good memory," I said.

"For faces, yes," he admitted, "but not for names."

"I am Samuel Plank, and this is William Wilson," I said.

"Last time you were here, I think you left with Alice – Miss Godfrey," he said. I listened for any threat or fear in his question, but there was none. And beside me Wilson smiled benignly.

"We did indeed," I replied. "We have mutual friends – the innkeepers at the Blue Boar, where Alice is lodging."

Buxton nodded, smiling. "And is Alice well? And the baby..." He frowned and shook his head.

"George," said Wilson.

"George," repeated Buxton. "That's it. A fine fellow. Although I suspect he will keep Alice from us for a while; they are demanding little creatures at that age, I seem to remember."

Our pleasantries exhausted, there was a short silence while the preacher looked at us questioningly.

"We have arrived early, Mr Buxton," I said, "because there is something we wanted to discuss with you before the meeting starts."

"Something religious?" asked Buxton. "Are you having a crisis of faith, or perhaps have questions about working for the Lord?" He looked at Wilson. "You would make a fine preacher, sir – very imposing."

I shook my head. "Nothing like that, no. Perhaps we should sit." Buxton looked from me to Wilson and back again and then sat on a bench. Wilson sat next to him while I took the bench opposite them. "You know," I continued, "we have another mutual friend. John Wontner, at Newgate."

"The keeper," said Buxton, and tapped his thigh. "Missing a leg."

"That's right," I said. "I understand you were in Newgate for three years, for publishing blasphemous materials."

"As with many things, my friend, blasphemy is a matter of perspective," said Buxton. "But yes, that was the charge, and I served my time under Mr Wontner's care. I've been more careful since, not to put anything on paper."

"So your beliefs remain the same as they were?" I asked.

Buxton looked at me appraisingly. "I hold that a man is entitled to his own beliefs, Samuel," he answered. "And now, perhaps, you could tell me why you have come here, as I doubt that it is for religious or moral debate."

"You are right, sir," I said, reaching into my pocket. "Mr Wilson and I are constables," I kept my eyes on his face as I said this, but he did not seem particularly perturbed by this revelation, "and we are concerned about two murders possibly connected with these meetings."

This time Buxton did react, and he looked genuinely startled. "Murders? But who?" he asked.

"The first is of a woman called Rose Welford, smothered by her husband of forty years," I said.

"Welford?" repeated Buxton. I nodded. He thought for a moment. "No, I do not know that name. Perhaps she came to only one meeting, and did not return."

"It is not the wife who came," I corrected, "but the husband. Josiah Welford." I waited, and Buxton thought again, but once more shook his head. "In that case," I continued, "do you know a man called Charlie Gordon? About my age, a scraggy sort of fellow, with a withered arm."

Buxton's face cleared. "Of course: Charlie has been a regular visitor for nigh on a year. He hasn't been at the last couple of meetings, but I assumed he was ill, or busy. I should have asked. Is he the second...?" I nodded, and he looked down and sighed. "I shall pray for his soul. Why was he murdered, constable? Something to do with his previous occupation?"

I ignored his question and instead laid on the table in front of him the greasy handbill that I had retrieved from Martha's basket. "You say that you are more careful these days, not to put anything in writing, Mr Buxton, and yet you – or your associates – are distributing these."

The preacher leaned over the handbill and read it carefully. He picked it up to look at the reverse, which was blank, and then read it again before turning to me.

"I am perplexed, constable," he said. "Where did you get this?"

"It was given to my wife when she attended a gathering at Cooper's Gardens," I explained. "It is not blasphemous, I do not think, but the reminder about the collection for the needy and destitute..."

"We make no collection, as you must know from your own visits," said Buxton. "If people are moved to donate money, we encourage them to spend it within their own community, to improve the lot of those around them."

"What about Eliza – did she collect money?" I asked.

"Eliza Mason? The herald?" asked Buxton. I nodded. "No: I paid her expenses myself – her food and travel."

"She was about to have a baby, was she not?" I asked.

"She was," replied Buxton. "And I am told that she was safely delivered. A little boy, I believe. One of the most gifted heralds – we miss her."

"She has not returned?" I asked.

Buxton shook his head. "I hoped she would, after her confinement, but she has not, no. There are others, of course, but the departed seem to come to Eliza more readily." He suddenly stopped and looked at me aghast. "Do you think something has happened to her – something connected with Charlie Gordon?"

"At the moment, Mr Buxton, I think many things," I said. I tapped the handbill with my finger. "If you do not collect money, why do you put this on your handbills?"

"I do not, constable," said Buxton. "I have never ordered or distributed handbills to solicit attendance at these meetings. Whoever has done so, it is without my request or even my knowledge."

Wilson and I sat in the Fox and French Horn on Clerkenwell Green, a tankard of ale apiece; we were about halfway home and, despite Martha's warning about my belly and ale, I had seen from the longing glances that Wilson cast at every tavern we passed that he was thirsty.

"Did you believe him?" asked Wilson, wiping the back of his hand across his mouth. "About the handbill and the collections, I mean – not about the heralds and the departed."

"I did, yes," I replied. "And you?" Wilson nodded. "What's more," I continued, "I liked him. A square fellow. I do not share his beliefs," Wilson frowned and shook his head, "but as long as he is not using those beliefs to cheat others, then I see no harm."

"No harm?" repeated Wilson. "But what about Mrs Welford? And Charlie Gordon?"

I held up my hand. "Now let's think about this carefully," I said. "You remember when we visited Mr Welford in Bethlem?" Wilson shuddered and nodded. "Do you have your notebook from that visit?"

"Aye," said Wilson, reaching into his pocket. "It's the same one I used just now with Buxton."

"Well, check back for me," I instructed. Wilson paged through his notebook until he reached the right page. "Didn't Welford say that his instructions to kill his wife had been passed to him at a special meeting?"

Wilson read his notebook. "That's it," he confirmed. "'Just me and a few of the brethren, and the herald.'" He looked up at me.

"And yet," I said, "the meetings we went to were crowded with people."

Wilson leaned forward. "Perhaps there are other meetings," he said. "And perhaps those meetings have nothing to do with Mr Buxton."

I nodded. "Mr Freame suggested the same thing – and that there is a careful selection of victims. Those who attend the gatherings at Cooper's Gardens and seem susceptible – vulnerable, perhaps – are encouraged to come to the meetings at the vinegar yard. And of them, the ones with something worth having – money, usually – are singled out for these special meetings. All very calculated. And cruel."

"But if it's not Buxton running the special meetings, who is it?" asked Wilson.

I drained my tankard and stood. "And now we've shown him the handbill, so he knows there's something going on. What might they do to him, if he starts asking questions?"

CHAPTER TWENTY-FOUR

Mr Buxton's bookings

MONDAY 20TH OCTOBER 1828

As I walked along Great Marlborough Street the next Monday, I was surprised to see Thin Billy – Mr Conant's valet – waiting at the foot of the steps leading to the magistrate's rooms above the court and offices. An indoor creature, Thin Billy was rarely seen outside, and he did not look comfortable. He spotted me coming towards him and beckoned me.

"Quickly, Sam, he's waiting for you," he said, leading me up the steps and opening the door for me. "Been here nearly an hour, and not himself at all."

"Miss Lily?" I asked as I climbed the stairs.

"No, more's the pity," said the valet. "She's staying with friends in Surrey, otherwise she could calm him down. As it is, you'll have to do." He stepped past me and opened the door, announcing me before hurrying away downstairs.

I walked into the room that served as dining room and office for John Conant. I usually found him sitting at his desk, reading papers or scratching hurried notes on them, but today he was standing by the fireplace, staring at his watch in his hand.

"Am I late, sir?" I asked.

"Late? Ah, no, not at all, constable," he replied. Constable, was it, rather than Sam – Thin Billy had been right about the magistrate's state of mind. "Tell me, constable," he continued, "just what is this hornets' nest you have been stirring?"

"Hornets' nest, sir?" I asked.

"This Buxton fellow," said Conant with exasperation. "The preacher."

"Ah," I said.

The magistrate shook his head and then pinched the bridge of his nose, as was his habit when something was on his mind. "For goodness' sake, Sam, sit down." He sat at his desk and waved me into another chair. "I take it that Buxton is connected with the religious gatherings you have attended, and the death of Charlie Gordon."

"Yes and no," I said. "Yes, John Buxton was the preacher at the meetings, but no, I don't think he had anything to do with Charlie's murder." I paused. "Might I ask, sir, why all of this has come to your attention again?"

"It seems that your Mr Buxton," said Conant, "is a popular man." He picked up a sheet of paper from his desk. "Now, remind me where the meetings were that you attended."

"Cooper's Gardens initially," I replied. "And latterly the vinegar yard in the City Road."

"Nowhere else?" asked the magistrate. I shook my head. He put on his spectacles and consulted the paper in his hand. "Well, in the last month alone, Mr Buxton was also booked to hold gatherings at the Blackfriars Rotunda, the Argyll Rooms and Almack's."

I raised my eyebrows. "Catering to the quality," I said.

"And the ladies of the quality are not used to being disappointed," said Conant. "When they are looking forward to an event and the man they have paid to see disappears, they complain to their husbands and their fathers and their brothers, and those husbands and fathers and brothers complain to me. Not all of them, of course, but enough. More than enough." He put down the paper and his spectacles and turned to me with a sigh. "And so I ask again, Sam: just what have you done?"

"Disappeared?" I asked. "John Buxton has disappeared?" A picture of Charlie Gordon lying in an alleyway with his throat cut came into my mind.

Conant looked again at the sheet of paper. "He was supposed to hold a gathering in the Rotunda last Thursday, and then one at Almack's on Saturday, and he missed them both. Others of his – what shall we call it – his organisation were there, including the young ladies who talk to the departed..."

"The heralds," I confirmed.

"The heralds. Indeed," said the magistrate, raising an eyebrow. "The herald was present on both evenings, but not Mr Buxton, and they declined to proceed without him."

"Might I ask, sir: did Miss Lily attend either of these gatherings?" I asked.

Conant shook his head. "She did not, no. She is in Godalming for a fortnight, with friends, but she would not have attended in any case. Since the incident at the home of Miss Palgrave, she has come to her senses and sees all of this," he gestured at the list of events, "for the masquerade that it is. What interests me is why Mr Buxton – with so much at stake – should choose this very moment to retire from public life."

"It may have something to do with me," I said. Conant looked levelly at me but said nothing. "Last Wednesday Constable Wilson and I went to see John Buxton; we called on him at the vinegar yard before one of his gatherings. I asked him about Charlie Gordon, and the heralds, and especially about the money that they raise from those who attend."

"Well, your questions were obviously a bit close to the bone," said the magistrate, "and your man has taken fright."

I shook my head. "I do not think he has taken fright, sir." I leaned forward. "I showed Buxton a handbill that had been used to promote his gatherings at the vinegar yard, and he said that he had distributed no such materials. He was adamant that he makes no collections at his gatherings. He knew nothing about Charlie Gordon, save that he had not seen him in recent weeks. And as we spoke he became concerned about one of his heralds – a young woman called Eliza Mason who was due to give birth and has not been seen since."

"With child?" asked Conant. "Like the girl who performed at the Palgrave house for Lily and her friends?"

I nodded. "I suspect it is the same girl, yes. Buxton was expecting her to return after her confinement, but she has not." I cleared my throat. "Which I think has a bearing on another matter. Concerning Alice Godfrey."

John Conant listened in silence as I told my tale, and when I had finished he shook his head sadly. "I have heard of such arrangements, of course," he said. "In even the finest families, an unexpected arrival for the daughter can be explained as a final flourish from the mother, with loyal servants assisting with the pretence. But that is done through love for those concerned, and a desire to shelter and care for them. This – this trade, well, that is something altogether different."

I nodded. "It smacks of the old system at the Foundling Hospital," I said.

"You mean when the governors of that institution resolved to receive only those children who were accompanied by substantial donations?" asked Conant.

"Indeed," I said grimly. "And before then, when Coram Men went around the country, offering – for a fee, of course – to take unwanted babies to the Hospital. Who knows how many of the poor mites survived that journey. It seems that whenever money is involved, it is the children who suffer."

"And you think that Buxton is running a trade in babies, and using his meetings to find buyers?" asked the magistrate.

I frowned. "It puzzles me, I will confess. I liked John Buxton. I thought him misguided but genuine in his beliefs, and a man of honourable feelings."

Conant smiled sadly. "But as you and I know only too well, Sam, the most successful old files are the most convincing ones. Those who are obvious rogues do not escape the shackles for long."

CHAPTER TWENTY-FIVE

Sophy's confession

TUESDAY 21ST OCTOBER 1828

I have worked since I was fourteen years old, and I believe that occupation is salvation. A man's work gives him not only food and shelter, but also pride and purpose. Idle hands and an empty mind soon fall prey to weakness and temptation and dark thoughts. And so when, after a good few weeks of keeping to herself as she mourned the loss of little Martha, my wife said that she would be returning to work at Mr Freame's school – as we called it in our house – I was relieved.

Set up with donations from members of the banker's Quaker community, the school equipped girls for a productive life as seamstresses, housekeepers and the like. Martha's role was to provide them with moral guidance – to alert them to the dangers and pitfalls of the world while demonstrating the happiness that can attend the making of good choices. She sometimes laughed at the very idea of herself as a teacher – she who could not read more than a few words until her husband taught her – but I knew from Mr Freame that she was respected and perhaps even loved by the girls under her care.

One evening soon after she had returned to the school, I came home to find Martha bristling as she prepared our meal, thumping lids onto pots and slamming plates onto the table. Wilson quickly took stock of the situation and suddenly remembered that he had promised to run an errand for his mother which would mean, sadly, that he could not join us. Martha pursed her lips but said nothing, and I envied him as he disappeared back into the night.

Indignation is a mood that Martha carries well, and tonight she was in full flow. I took off my coat, rinsed my hands and face, and sat at the table as she bustled around me. I knew better than to prompt her, as this would only make me the focus of her annoyance, and so I shook out the evening newspaper and feigned interest in its headlines.

"If you want something sensational to read," said Martha tartly, "take a look at this." She reached into the pocket of her apron and took out a sheet of paper. She unfolded it, slapped it onto the table and shoved it towards me.

"Another handbill?" I said.

She tutted. "What's the point of me telling you, when you've eyes in your head to read it yourself." She waited until I had started reading and then turned to the stove.

"The Awful Disclosures of Sophy Saunders," I read. "The full and terrible story of how I was misled and cruelly abandoned by a man of few morals and great wickedness." I looked up at my wife's back. "I hope you didn't pay a good penny for this nonsense, Mar," I said.

"I did not, no," she replied. "I confiscated it from one of the girls, but by then it had already been passed around the school." She pulled out a chair and sat down, sighing heavily.

"It's not like you to take something like this so seriously," I said, reaching over to take her hand. "All young girls – and probably lads too – like a bit of gossip. And at least it means they're reading."

Martha looked at me sharply. "It's not the fact of the thing, Sam. As you say, I've caught girls with them before. I would have liked them myself at their age, if I'd had a penny to spare – or if I could have read them. No, read on." She tapped the paper with her finger and then sat back with her arms folded. "This one is a bit different."

I did read on. And as I did, I felt a chill. Miss Saunders explained how she was working as a kitchen maid in a grand house just north of London, where she fell in love with one of the grooms. They hoped to marry, but before they could make good on their plans, he died in an accident. Heartbroken, Sophy attended a religious gathering and there she fell under the spell of a man who claimed that he could contact her dead love for her. Her hopes kept alive by occasional messages that her groom sent her from beyond the grave, she followed this man to London. There she had no protectors, and she was pressed into service by the man who had led her astray – first as his mistress, and then as a herald, as he taught her the secrets of communicating with the departed. When she told him that she was with child, he forced her to have the baby and then give it away so that she could continue her work with him. None of this shook her devotion to him, but when she discovered that he had another two mistresses, as well as a wife and three children at home, she finally saw the light and was writing this, her story and her confession, as a warning to other young women.

I looked up at Martha.

"It's Buxton, isn't it?" she asked sadly. "This Sophy Saunders – she's just like Eliza, isn't she? A herald. Except that it's all a trick."

I stood and walked over to my wife and crouched down beside her chair. "I'm sorry, Mar," I said.

She shook her head and blinked a few times. With one hand she scrabbled in her pocket, and I silently handed her my handkerchief. She wiped fiercely at her eyes.

"You knew, didn't you?" she asked. "You knew it was all a fraud. That the girls were just making it up."

I looked up at her. "I suspected, yes," I admitted.

"And William?" asked Martha.

"We both suspected," I replied.

"And you were laughing at me all this time," she said bitterly. "Laughing at poor, bird-witted Martha, too ignorant to know when she's being gulled."

I reached around the table and pulled my chair towards me. I sat on it, next to Martha, and held out my hands. After a minute, she reluctantly put her hands in mine and I stroked the back of them with my thumbs.

"Not for one second, my dearest girl," I said. "My heart ached for you, to think that you needed such comfort. And if it were just messages devised to bring peace to people, then, well, I would not take it from you for the world. But there is more to it than that, and I cannot protect you without telling you the truth. And the truth has hurt you, for which I am more sorry than I can say." I bent my head and kissed Martha's hands in turn. "And you were not foolish or silly, my dear. Mr Buxton is a credible man because he deserves to be."

Martha looked at me. "What do you mean, Sam?"

"I mean that I think that Mr Buxton is a good and genuine man of honest Christian beliefs," I said. I told her what I had found out at Newgate, and how Buxton had been as bemused as me by the handbill and its reference to collections, and finally about the preacher's disappearance. "I talked to him and I liked him," I said, "and I think that he is as much a victim of this fraud as everyone else at those meetings. I believe that even more so, now that he has gone missing. And, as you know, I am never wrong."

That did the trick; a small – a very small – smile started to appear, and Martha squeezed my hand. I reached up and very gently wiped a tear from her cheek.

"Will you go to the vinegar yard tomorrow, my dear?" I asked.

Martha shook her head. "It would not be the same," she said. "And I think perhaps I have been out too often in the evenings in recent weeks. Who knows what mischief you get up to without me here to keep an eye on you."

"Ah well, I shall have to send a message to cancel the dancing girls," I said, "but perhaps it's for the best."

CHAPTER TWENTY-SIX

The printer in Chequer Yard

WEDNESDAY 22ND OCTOBER 1828

The next morning, Martha was quiet as she set my breakfast before me. She had been restless in the night, but I had not pestered her with questions. When someone has been tricked, the damage to their dignity can take as long to heal as a physical injury. I ate, and then caught her hand as she reached for my empty plate and pulled her onto my lap; she did not resist but just looked at me sadly.

"I'll find out what I can today," I said to her. "About Mr Buxton. I know you are worried about him."

"But be careful, Sam," she said. "Maybe you are wrong about him. Maybe he has fooled both of us. Maybe he is involved in everything – Charlie Gordon, Alice's baby, everything. He's a good preacher, after all. And good preachers can persuade people to do and believe all sorts of things. Even you."

It saddened me to see Martha so mistrustful but she was right; maybe Buxton's innocence and outrage had all been feigned. And now that he had disappeared, I could not challenge him. I saw that the awful disclosures of Miss Saunders were still on the table – Martha must have been re-reading them. I reached for the handbill, and noticed that the printer had added his name to the bottom of the sheet, so that people would know where to buy more copies. "Printed at the Catnach Press, 2 and 3 Monmouth Court, Seven Dials, London – Printed cheap", it said. It gave me an idea.

"In the pocket of my coat, Mar," I said, pointing. "The handbill that you were given at Cooper's Gardens – the one I showed to Buxton."

Martha stood and went to my coat, bringing the folded handbill to me. I opened it out and checked at the bottom of the page. Yes, there it was again: "Printed by W Heseltine, Printer, Chequer Yard, Dowgate Hill, London".

Buxton had been adamant that he had known nothing of the handbill soliciting donations from those who attended his meetings. Perhaps the printer could prove him right or wrong.

"Dowgate Hill?" asked Wilson as we walked down Cleveland Street.

"In the city," I said, "just past St Paul's."

Wilson stopped on the spot. "All that way?" he said.

"And you with your young legs," I said. "Less than an hour, and I daresay we will pass a pie seller or two on the way."

And indeed it was just on the hour as we turned off Cannon Street – particularly busy at this time of day – and into the much narrower Dowgate Hill, threading down towards the river. The grand pale frontage of Skinners' Hall was on our right, and we had frequently to step to the side to allow carts past as they carried cargoes to and from Dowgate Wharf. Turnwheel Lane added to the traffic, and then on the left we spotted Chequer Yard, even narrower, and cast into permanent shadow by the tall buildings on either side. We passed another livery hall – the plumbers', I think – and a cotton merchant, and any number of crowded warehouses, and finally came to the premises of the printer. We knocked on the door and there was no reply, but we could hear someone inside. I pulled the door open and we stepped in.

It was a tiny space, almost completely filled by a two identical black metal printing presses. Stacks of paper covered every available surface and most of the floor, while wooden drying racks – similar to those used for laundry – were suspended from the ceiling and draped with yet more paper. Standing between the presses was a lad of about fourteen, wearing a black-stained apron that reached to the ground and went around him twice, and so engrossed was he in his work that we were able to watch him unobserved for a few minutes. He would turn the handle of one press to raise the weight and slide out the plate, dab on some fresh ink with a cloth sponge, twirl the handle again, and then – seemingly with all his weight – force a last rotation of the handle to make the impression. Then he would turn his attention to the other press and go through the same routine before going back to the first press and raising the plate to remove the printed sheet. It was rather like a dance, so carefully timed were his movements. The air was filled with the tangy, metallic smell of the ink.

"Good morning," I called out, but the lad ignored us. "You there," I tried again, but there was no response. Wilson made to step forward but just then the lad caught sight of us and stopped. He reached to the floor by his feet and picked up a hand-bell, which he clanged loudly. Wilson looked at me in alarm. A door at the back of the room opened and a much older man appeared, wiping his hands on his own apron. The lad grunted loudly and pointed at us, then returned to his work. The man picked his way across the room, stepping nimbly over the piles of paper, until he reached me and held out his hand.

"Welcome, gentlemen," he said. "How may I be of assistance?"

"Your lad," I said, nodding towards the boy, who once again had his back to us and was fully engaged in his dance with the presses.

"Deaf," said the man. "Since birth, they tell me. Have you heard of the asylum in Old Kent Road, the one for deaf and dumb children?" I shook my head. "Marvellous, it is. Teaches them to read and write, and sometimes to speak – although I'm not fussy on that score. Lots of printers get their lads from there now, especially the big ones using steam-powered presses."

"Because they're not disturbed by the noise," said Wilson.

"Precisely," said the printer. "If he's a quick study – like Jenkins over there – so much the better. There's not many can run two machines as well as he can." He glanced at my coat. "How can I help you, constable?"

I took the handbill out of my pocket and handed it to him. "Do you recognise this?" I asked.

He looked at the paper and nodded. "It's one of ours, as of course you know. There's my name at the bottom: William Heseltine. We do dozens like it every week." He handed it back to me.

"Can you remember who ordered it?" I asked.

"Let me think. Well, it was a tall man," he replied. "Taller than your young fellow here. About seven foot,

I'd say – maybe eight. With bright red hair, oh, and only one arm. Should be easy to find." He winked at Wilson, who crossed out the words he had just written in his notebook. "No, I don't remember – but it will be in my ledger. Wait here."

The printer walked back through his shop and disappeared into his office.

"Quite the joker, isn't he," said Wilson, much on his dignity.

"We meet enough people in a bad humour," I said. "A bit of levity now and then does not go amiss. He meant no harm by it." But there are few who take themselves more seriously than a young man in the execution of his duty, and Wilson simply sniffed dismissively.

The door of the office opened and Mr Heseltine came out carrying a large ledger. He carried it over to us, rested it on top of a pile of paper and opened it.

"Given the dates shown on the handbill, it would have been ordered sometime in this fortnight…" he said quietly, turning pages and running his finger down the entries. "May I see it again?" I placed the handbill on the ledger and he checked it. "Yes, here we go." He pointed to a line in the ledger. "Order placed Monday 21st July, collected Monday 28th July. Five hundred copies. Paid in full. Mr Buxton."

I looked at Wilson who was taking notes. "Buxton – you are sure of that?" I asked.

The printer looked again at the ledger. "Certain: it's in my own writing. Here, see for yourself: Mr Francis Buxton."

CHAPTER TWENTY-SEVEN

A sorry end

THURSDAY 23RD OCTOBER 1828 – MORNING

"Francis Buxton?" asked Mr Conant. "Not John?"

As soon as Wilson and I had arrived at Great Marlborough Street, I had gone up to the magistrate's dining room to tell him what we had learned the previous day.

"Perhaps his full name is Francis John, or John Francis," I suggested. "With a criminal record, he might choose to use different names in different places. Or it may be a mistake, with the printer writing down the wrong name."

"Well, it seems to me that you have to put these options to Mr Buxton, which means that you need to find him," said the magistrate, removing his spectacles and rubbing the red patches they had left on the sides of his nose. "Unless you have another suggestion?"

But before I had time to consider my answer, there was an urgent knocking at the door and Wilson looked into the room.

"Excuse me, sir," he said, "but we're needed in the front office. Right now, sir, if you can."

"Off you go, Sam," said the magistrate. "You can tell me more later."

I followed Wilson down the stairs and up the outside steps into the front office. Standing by the counter, hopping impatiently from foot to foot and twisting his hat in his hands, was the message lad Jimmy. Since he had been rewarded so generously after the discovery of Charlie Gordon's body, he had made it his business to stick to the streets around Great Marlborough Street so as to be first in line for any service that Wilson or I might need. As soon as he saw us, he beckoned us into a corner of the front office, looking mistrustfully over his shoulder at office-keeper Tom Neale. Tom caught my eye, winked, and made himself scarce on some errand to the back office.

After checking once more for any eavesdroppers, Jimmy leaned towards us and whispered, "There's another one. Another body. Same place as the other one, same..." He drew a finger across his throat to indicate the cause of death. "But this one," he swallowed, "it's a girl."

We looked down at the body. Just as last time, it was leaning against the wall of the same alley in Carnaby Market, far enough from the main thoroughfare that passersby would not spot it. As Jimmy had said, there was the same wound across the throat, but this time – and I tried not to show my relief at this – there was no label around the neck. She was about eighteen, I estimated, with a round face and dark red hair coiled up but coming loose, probably from the struggle when she was attacked. She was dressed neatly enough in a green dress and dark shawl – perhaps a seamstress or a housemaid, judging by the cleanliness of her hands and face, and the neatness of her fingernails. Certainly not a Covent Garden nun. I ordered Wilson and Jimmy to turn their backs and then lifted her skirt to check for injury; there was none.

"How did you find her, Jimmy?" I asked, rearranging her skirt to cover her.

He answered without turning around. "Since the last one, I always check this alley. Don't know why – I just had a feeling."

I stood and went over to him, putting a hand on his shoulder. "You did well, lad," I said.

Jimmy turned and beamed; I doubt that praise comes his way too often. "Did you see the paper, Mr Plank?" he asked.

"Paper?" I repeated. "What paper?"

"In her hand – that one," he said, pointing. "And I think there's one in her mouth. You can just see the corner of it, but I didn't want to, well, touch her."

I crouched and looked again at the woman's body. Jimmy was right: she was clutching a piece of paper screwed up in her right hand. I uncurled her fingers and removed the paper.

"Wilson," I said, "come and hold her head for me."

Wilson squatted down next to me and swallowed hard before taking hold of the woman's head. He closed his eyes and the colour drained from his face. I carefully put my fingers into the mouth and managed to open the jaw sufficiently to pull out the paper corner that Jimmy had seen; I couldn't release the whole thing, but tore off about half of it. Wilson made a strange gurgling noise, suggesting he was about to cast up his account.

"Quick," I said. "Get out into the fresh air."

He did as I said, as I carefully covered the body in the horse blanket that once again we had brought from the office. Jimmy agreed to stand watch until we could have the body collected by a coroner and Wilson and I walked slowly back towards Great Marlborough Street, with him taking deep breaths. We climbed the steps of the courthouse and walked through to the back office, with me indicating to Tom that he should bring us a hot drink.

"The special?" he asked, casting a practiced eye at Wilson's pallor. I nodded, and knew that the teapot would benefit from a generous slug of brandy before it reached us. In the back office we sat down; Wilson leaned on the table, hunched over his clasped hands, and looked across at me.

"I am sorry," he said quietly. "It's not the first corpse I have seen – far from it. But something about her..."

"Wilson," I said, "it is to your credit that you cannot look on such horror with ease. It is not a sign of weakness to feel compassion or revulsion. I would be more concerned if you were unaffected."

Tom came in with the tray and poured us each a mug of steaming tea. Wilson took a gulp of his and his eyes widened in surprise.

"Drink up, lad," said Tom as he left us. "Constable's orders."

I blew on my drink and sipped more cautiously. "Now, if you are feeling revived," I said, "we can look at these papers."

I took them out of my pocket – the crumpled complete sheet and the torn piece. I straightened them both out and we leaned forward to look at them. They were both copies of the same handbill: The Awful Disclosures of Sophy Saunders.

Back upstairs in the magistrate's dining room, Mr Conant looked at the handbills and then up at us.

"And you think that the murdered girl is Sophy Saunders?" he asked.

"As sure as we can be," I said. "The handbills left with the body," I pointed at the papers, "have the name of the printer at the bottom of them. Constable Wilson was in need of fresh air and something to occupy his mind, so I sent him off to speak to the printer – Mr Catnach, at Seven Dials – and one of the printer's lads recognised her from the description. They spent quite a bit of time together, Sophy and the printer's lad, while she told him the story and he set it for printing. She was a pretty thing." I sighed. "But she spoke out of turn and was punished for it. Leaving the handbill in her mouth is meant, I am sure, as a warning to others who might be thinking of talking."

"Poor girl," said Conant, shaking his head. "What a life – and what an end to it."

CHAPTER TWENTY-EIGHT

A familiar face

THURSDAY 23RD OCTOBER 1828 – EVENING

My walk home that evening was troubled. On the one hand, I did not want to tell Martha about the murder of Sophy Saunders; it was an upsetting, gruesome death that would frighten and disturb her. But on the other, I knew that keeping it from her would be both difficult and dangerous. Women will often – surprisingly often – forgive bad behaviour, but they are much less forgiving of secrets. I had still not decided on my course of action when I arrived home, thinking that Martha's mood might suggest the best approach. I was just pushing the door open to go into the kitchen when Martha's face appeared in the gap.

"Hold on, Sam," she whispered. "Are you alone, or is William with you?" She peered past me and I looked over my shoulder like a villain in a pantomime. She tutted.

"I think I'm alone, Mar," I whispered back.

"Then you can come in," she said, opening the door a little more, "but you have to promise me that you will listen carefully before you lose your temper."

"Am I going to lose my temper, then?" I asked, taking off my coat and hanging it on the hook. "Have you burnt the dinner? Decided to run off with the coal man?"

"And which of those two would bother you more, I wonder," she said. "I'm serious, Sam: there's someone here to see you, and it's taken a lot of courage for him to come at all, so don't you frighten him off. And you'll need this." She reached into the pocket of my coat and handed me my notebook.

Martha led me into the sitting room. A man was perched on the edge of my armchair and leapt to his feet when he heard the door open. As he turned to greet me, I recognised him: it was the queer plunger from the Green Park reservoir.

"This is Mr Keane," she said, indicating our visitor, "and this is my husband, Constable Plank."

Keane held out his hand and I shook it. "Tobias Keane, sir," he said.

"Sam Plank," I replied, indicating that he should sit. He waited until I had taken the other chair and then sat down again. Martha raised an eyebrow at me as she returned to the kitchen, pulling the door closed behind her.

"You are a good deal drier than when I saw you last," I observed.

He nodded but had no breath to speak. He reached into his pocket for a handkerchief and coughed into it before wiping his lips. "I am, sir, yes, but paying a price for all that time spent in cold water."

"Indeed," I said. "I am surprised to see you in my home, Mr Keane. If you have something to discuss concerning your work or mine, why did you not call to see me at Great Marlborough Street?"

"After what happened to Charlie..." he coughed again, this time for longer. I waited. "After that," he continued, "I can't be seen going into a police office. More than my life is worth." There was another bout of coughing. Martha came back into the room and wordlessly put a tumbler of water on the hearth at Keane's feet. "Thanks, missus," he said breathlessly.

"What you need is white horehound," she replied. "Pour hot water on the leaves, leave them to steep, and drink the liquid. Morning, noon and night." She returned to the kitchen.

Keane looked at me as he drank the water, and I nodded. "She knows her plants, does Mrs Plank," I confirmed. "Kept me hale and hearty for a quarter-century."

"Charlie said you could be trusted." Keane sat back a little as he said this and looked at me appraisingly.

"I'm glad to hear it," I replied. "Although I can't say that I felt the same way about him."

Keane smiled and shook his head. "Charlie was a rogue, that's true, but not a wicked man." A shadow came across his face. "He didn't deserve what they did to him, sir."

"That I can agree with," I said, "from what I knew of Charlie. What I don't know is who killed him." I looked at Keane. "Were you there?"

He shook his head. "I was supposed to be, but I did not have the heart for it. I sent word that I was cropsick." He coughed again. "I hoped they might delay, that Buxton might think better of it..."

"But there are always those willing to do the Devil's work for a few coins," I finished for him. He nodded. I opened my notebook and looked across at him. He paused for a moment and then nodded again. "Buxton, you said," I continued. "John Buxton?"

Keane barked with laughter. "The Devil's work – John Buxton? He's working for the other master – although much good may it do him, with a brother like that. Francis Buxton, now: he could teach the Devil a trick or two."

Brothers. John and Francis Buxton were brothers. "What sort of tricks?" I asked.

"Deception. Thieving. Murder," said Keane with bitterness.

"Deception?" I prompted, writing the word in my book and underlining it.

"Well, you've seen it yourself," he said. I looked up at him. "Aye, I saw you there, constable, at the vinegar yard," he continued, a half-smile on his face. "You're not the only one who keeps an eye out for what he can see. The herald, I mean. Talking to the departed. All that nonsense."

"But that was John Buxton, not Francis," I said. "As you say, I've seen it myself. And the only brother I saw was John."

Keane leaned forward. "That's the genius of it all," he said. "Francis takes care not to be seen. Not in public, anyway. He does not have his brother's charm. John – well, you've heard him. He has the gift of words: people hear him and they like him and they believe him. Francis is an altogether harder fellow – rough, and sharp. Years ago he realised that he could use John to snare victims, to coax them into his trap."

"And does John Buxton not mind?" I asked, thinking of the honest-seeming man I had met.

"John Buxton does not know," replied Keane.

I looked up in surprise. "He does not know that he is doing his brother's bidding?" I asked.

Keane shook his head. "He's as much of a gull as the rest of them, sitting on their benches, waiting to hear from their dead. You saw Eliza?"

"The herald – the one who had the baby?" I confirmed. "Yes, I saw her."

"Well, the chit is almost certainly Francis Buxton's bastard," said Keane. "Eliza has been his mistress for two years now."

I thought of little George, and the love in Alice's eyes as she had gazed at him in her arms.

Keane continued. "It was Eliza who convinced John Buxton that she could talk to the departed. She told him that his mother – he was very fond of his mother – wanted to pass on a message to him. He didn't believe her at first – what God-fearing man would? But then she started telling him things that only his mother would know – his pet-name when he was a boy, that sort of thing – and gradually he was taken in. Reeled in. She wasn't speaking to the dear departed Mrs Buxton, of course: someone else was giving her the information she needed to convince him." He looked at me. "Someone else who would know those things."

"His brother Francis," I finished.

Keane nodded.

"And have you known this all along?" I asked.

Keane shifted in his seat and had the good grace to blush a little. "As long as I've been working for Buxton – Francis, that is – yes." He paused and I waited, my pencil poised above my notebook. He cleared his throat. "My job was to find out more about the people who came to the meetings at the vinegar yard. Another fellow handed out handbills at Cooper's Gardens, and then once they turned up at John Buxton's meetings, I had to find out who they were and whether they had money. If they did, I would invite them to a different meeting, more private – a special meeting for the chosen ones, we told them."

"And who would attend that meeting?" I asked.

"Francis and Eliza, always," said Keane. "Usually three other men – friends of Francis, who would agree with whatever he said."

"Not John Buxton?" I asked.

"Of course not, constable," said Keane. "He knew nothing about this side of… the business. Knows nothing."

"And at this special meeting, what would the victim be told?" I asked.

Keane shrugged and coughed again. "Whatever Buxton needed to tell them to get their money, I suppose. I was not there myself – only men who could be taken for preachers were in attendance. And I don't have the look of the hum box about me, do I?" Taking note of his battered features and shabby clothes, I had to agree.

"But you heard about the special meetings?" I asked.

"People talk," he said.

"Did you hear about Josiah Welford?" I asked.

Keane looked down at the floor and nodded.

"You know then that he murdered his wife, on the basis of instructions that he was given at one of Buxton's special meetings?" I asked.

He nodded again.

"And you know that he is now in Bethlem, and likely to remain there for the rest of his days?" I continued.

This time Keane shook his head and looked up at me with great sadness. "I am sorry to hear it." He took a deep breath that turned into another coughing fit. I waited. He finished coughing and breathed raggedly for a minute or two before speaking. "This is why I have come to you, constable. It has gone too far now. When it was just money, that was one thing. Money can be replaced. But now there is murder, and madness."

"And you are scared for your own life," I said quietly.

"God forgive my cowardice, but yes," he replied. "Can you help me, constable?"

I cannot explain it, but somehow I knew that Martha was standing outside the closed door, her ear to the panel, holding her breath and waiting for my answer.

"I can make no guarantees, Mr Keane," I said. I leaned forward in my seat and beckoned him to do likewise. I lowered my voice. "But I have an offer to make to you." I looked at him and he nodded. I continued in low tones. "I need to find out more about Francis Buxton and his methods. Can you help me find a way into his ken? I want to see him at work."

Keane swallowed hard; his fear of Buxton and his men was not feigned. "And what do you offer me in return, constable?" he asked quietly.

"When I have what I need," I replied, and now I raised my voice again to normal pitch, "I can have a strong young constable escort you out of London – you have somewhere else to go? Other skills?"

"My grandfather was a farmer, in the West Country," he replied. "I know a little of the care of cattle, and I have relations there still."

"Then I suggest you return to them," I said. "If you stay in London, there is little I can do for you. You will almost certainly end up like Charlie Gordon."

Keane closed his eyes for a few seconds and shuddered. Then he looked at me and pointed to my notebook. "And what will you tell the magistrates?" he asked. "I am involved, after all. Will I be a wanted man?"

"The information you have given me will be invaluable," I said, "and I shall certainly tell the magistrates that it is sound information passed to me by a reliable source. But that source is, as anyone can see from my notes," I paged back through the book, "unnamed."

Keane's shoulders slumped. "Thank you, sir," he said quietly.

The door opened and Martha looked into the room.

"Dinner is almost ready, Sam," she said.

Keane stood up. He held out his hand and I shook it. He walked into the kitchen, where Martha handed him a package.

"Bread, some cheese, a slice of ham pie and a piece of walnut loaf," she explained. "To see you on your way to the West Country. And this," she gave him a small wrap of brown paper, "is horehound leaves."

Keane took the items from Martha and ducked his head in thanks.

"'Tis very kind of you, missus," he said.

Martha nodded. "We're none of us perfect, Mr Keane. But you are trying to make amends, and that is important. I wish you Godspeed."

CHAPTER TWENTY-NINE

The caretaker's storeroom

THURSDAY 30TH OCTOBER 1828

Wilson stood before the door of the back office, his arms folded and a mulish look on his face. I checked the pockets of my coat – a plain and shabby one borrowed from Tom Neale's storeroom – to make sure that I had nothing on me to identify me as a constable and walked towards Wilson.

"Out of the way, now, lad," I said. "I have an appointment to keep, and if I am late, Keane may well lose his nerve and scarper."

Wilson shook his head firmly, just the once. "I'm sorry, sir, no."

"Your concern for me does you credit, constable," I said, "but this scheme is of my making. I cannot – I will not – drag you into it. These are dangerous men."

Wilson frowned at me. "Do you think that I became a constable for the easy life and the gold buttons on the coat? That I am chicken-hearted?"

I smiled, which only made him frown all the harder – I had forgotten how easily bruised is the young man's pride.

"You are far from chicken-hearted, Wilson," I said. "But when you go into danger, you risk more than your own life: you have a mother and siblings who depend entirely upon you."

"And you, sir," he said, "you have Mrs Plank who depends entirely upon you."

I shook my head. "That is not so. If I were dead, she would turn to friends – to Mr Freame, and to Mr Wontner and Mr Conant, and to you."

"And my mother, she would turn to you, and to Mr Neale, and to others here in the office." Wilson looked at me challengingly. "I know the risks, sir, and I accept them. I am grateful for your care, but I would be a poor constable if I shirked any of my duties through fear for my personal safety. And I will not be a poor constable, sir." He could see my hesitation, and played his trump card. "Or perhaps you would prefer me to go and wait with Mrs Plank, to make sure that she is not too worried about you."

"Hah!" I said. "As well you know, I have given Mrs Plank no reason to be worried about my movements this evening."

"Then it would be a shame for her to find out," Wilson replied with satisfaction.

I held up my hands in surrender. "Ask Tom if he has another coat you can wear."

"Already done," said Wilson, opening the door and heading to the front office.

The office-keeper handed him a long, dark coat with mud splashes on the hem.

"The previous owner has no further need of it," Tom explained. "Came to an untimely end in a brawl outside the Bricklayer's Arms. The bigger they are, the harder they fall. But there's a silver lining to every cloud, and now Constable Wilson can look every inch the ruffian."

I raised an eyebrow at the office-keeper. "You knew that he would be coming with me, it seems."

"I did," said Tom stoutly. "It was only you that needed persuading."

It took us almost an hour in the falling darkness to walk to the place that Keane had specified: the White Hart, on the corner of Old Street Road and Bunhill Row. The tavern was only a matter of yards from the vinegar yard, and the by now familiar briny smell filled the air. Wilson pushed open the door to the bar and stood aside to let me go in first. It was dim and smoky, and we stood for a moment in the doorway. Once I could see clearly again, I looked around the room for Keane. A man of his experience, and particularly one afeared for his life, would select his seat carefully. And indeed, I spotted him at a small table in a corner, his back to the wall, and with a good view of both the main door through which we had entered, and the back door leading to the yard. He had seen me before I saw him, and from his expression I could tell he was displeased.

We walked over to his table, signalling to the tavern keeper for three tankards of ale. Ordinarily I was cautious about drinking while on duty, and indeed tried to instil the same habit into Wilson, but on the way to our destination I had explained to him that we needed to put Keane at his ease. I also had in mind that the men I hoped he would take us to might trust us more if we smelt of the tavern. Wilson was quite happy to fall in with this new plan.

We arrived at Keane's table and he looked up at us, the scowl still on his face.

"You said you'd come alone," he said to me, jerking his head towards Wilson. "Who's this? Your fart catcher?"

Wilson took a step closer to the table, but just then the potboy arrived with our drinks and I took the opportunity to sit down, indicating that Wilson should do the same. I leaned in towards Keane.

"This is Constable Wilson," I said quietly. "Given what you have told me about your crew, I thought an extra pair of fists on our side might not go amiss."

Keane looked at Wilson, who stared back at him. They both lifted their tankards and took a deep draught, never once taking their eyes off each other. Keane put his tankard on the table and wiped the back of his hand across his mouth.

"Perhaps you're right," he said.

"He's right," said Wilson.

"We'll find out soon enough, gentlemen," I said, taking a mouthful of my own ale. "Unless you have summoned me all the way out to Shoreditch just to test my resolve, Mr Keane."

Keane was in the middle of draining his tankard, but he shook his head. "Buxton likes to keep things close to home," he said. "And round here he has everything he needs. Premises, bolt-holes, loyal men – and constables he can grease in the fist. That's partly why I went so far afield to find you, Mr Plank – that, and I know Charlie Gordon liked you. He didn't like many, Charlie." He was silent for a few moments as he thought of his friend.

"Well now, Mr Keane," I said eventually. "Perhaps you could take us to Mr Buxton."

We walked back out onto Old Street Road and turned eastwards. Wilson tapped me on the shoulder and pointed to a sign high on the wall behind us, indicating the name of the narrow alley running down the side of the tavern: Martha's Buildings. I smiled to think that she was watching over us, even if she did not know it. On the other side of the road, behind an imposing wall, was a very grand building made of red brick, with a columned frontage several hundred feet long consisting of a central pedimented entrance and two symmetrical wings.

"It reminds me of Bethlem," I observed to Wilson.

"As well it might," said Keane, looking across at it with a shudder. "That's St Luke's – another madhouse." He started walking quickly towards the crossroads with the City Road, where the vinegar yard occupied the north-east corner. Opposite the vinegar yard was another elegant structure, much smaller than St Luke's but with pleasing proportions, plenty of windows and a graceful tower: lettering across the front, above the entrance, told us that this was the City of London Lying-in Hospital.

"Plenty of that sort of thing around here," said Keane, catching me looking at the building. "A couple of streets north there's the French Hospital. Rich pickings, if you're looking for the bereaved. He's no fool, Francis Buxton."

At City Road we paused for a coach to go past and then crossed at an angle, heading south.

"Down here," said Keane, leading us off the main road.

"Tabernacle Row," said Wilson, glancing at the sign. "Like the tabernacle in the Bible?"

Keane shrugged. He stopped and looked back past us towards City Road, and then checked up and down the street a couple of times. When he was satisfied that no-one else was nearby, he knocked on the door of a brick building: two short knocks, then one long, then three short. We heard footsteps coming towards us and the door was opened a crack, spilling light from a lantern into the street. Keane leaned towards the gap and the lantern was lifted to illuminate his face. Satisfied, the holder of the lantern opened the door wider so that we could enter. He was an old fellow, obviously a caretaker of some sort, wearing a long coat with a shawl over his shoulders; he looked a bit surprised to see three of us, but Keane nodded to him and handed him a small purse, and he led us into the gloom. We walked along a corridor, with closed doors along its length.

Keane glanced back over his shoulder. "Schoolrooms," he said.

The caretaker reached the end of the corridor and opened a door which led out into the schoolyard. Tall terraces loomed over us, surrounding the small space allowed to the schoolchildren for recreation. Across the yard was a wooden outbuilding built against the wall; the caretaker walked to the door of it and turned to hand his lantern to Keane, who lifted it so that the caretaker could examine his bunch of keys and select the one he needed to unlock the door. This done, the lantern was handed back, and the caretaker ushered us all into the outbuilding. In the swinging light of the lantern I could see boxes and cases, tools and pots; this was plainly the caretaker's storeroom. He walked to the back wall of the building and turned his lantern down low before putting it on a shelf and retrieving from the same place a long knife. He then bent slightly and, using first the knife and then the tips of his fingers, removed a single small brick. He put it carefully on the shelf and then stood to one side. Keane put his finger to his lips and then indicated that I should look through the gap.

At first I could see nothing, but then I realised that I was looking into a room. The storeroom had been built to take advantage of the back wall of another building, and now I was looking directly into that building. It was a dimly lit room, with a grate at one side which was burning low. There were three chairs that I could see, although as I was looking through such a small gap I could not tell what was near our shared wall. Against the wall opposite the fire was a low bed, and reclining on this was a half-dressed woman. The firelight was kind to her, but even with this blessing I could tell that she was a bawd. I stood back from the wall and looked at Keane, raising my eyebrow. He held up a hand, telling me to wait, and then pointed at his eye. I looked again through the gap.

The door to the room opened and in came a man. It had to be Francis Buxton. He shared his brother's build and his dark, curling hair, but whereas John's features were open and kind, those of Francis had hardened into sharpness and mistrust – and cruelty. He went over to the bed and looked down at the woman. She lifted her arms beckoningly but he took rough hold of her wrists and hauled her upright. She grabbed a blanket from the bed and tried to cover herself as he pushed her towards the door.

"Get out," I heard him say.

Now alone, Buxton bent down and banked up the fire. Then he picked up one of the chairs and positioned it so that it was facing the other two. There was a knock at the door and in walked a woman whom I recognised. I turned my head towards Wilson.

"It's Eliza – the herald," I whispered.

"A special meeting, then," said Keane. "They've scented money."

There was another knock and this time Buxton went to the door and held out his hand to welcome the visitor. It was another woman, aged about sixty, whose fine silk skirts gleamed in the firelight. With much care and deference, Buxton showed her to one of the chairs and sat down beside her. Eliza sat opposite them and held out her hand. At Buxton's bidding, the older woman placed her hand in Eliza's; her other hand rested on the velvet reticule in her lap. I turned my head to put my ear to the gap, but the little group was so tightly huddled that I could make out little of what was said. Eliza had her eyes closed, and at one point she flung out her arms, making the older woman snatch back her own hand in alarm. Buxton leaned towards his visitor and spoke quietly, which seemed to reassure her.

After about ten minutes, Eliza opened her eyes and looked about her in the manner of one woken from sleep. The older woman sat transfixed, staring at her. She reached into her reticule and brought out a handkerchief to dab at her eyes. Eliza stood and walked past the woman towards the door, but the woman put out a hand to stop her, as Buxton had obviously intended. The visitor dipped again into her reticule and this time brought out a small purse which she handed to Eliza, smiling up into her face. Eliza took the purse and touched the woman's shoulder, as though in blessing. The woman stood, bade farewell to Buxton and Eliza, and left the room. Buxton closed the door behind her and held out his hand. Eliza passed the purse to him and he took it and smiled. Eliza did not smile in return.

CHAPTER THIRTY

A woman of quality

FRIDAY 31ST OCTOBER 1828

"A woman of quality, you think?" asked John Conant the next morning, as I made my report to him.

"Without a doubt," I replied. "I should think it will be a gradual process, her fleecing. The purse she gave them yesterday was small, but there's plenty more where that came from, judging from her appearance."

"And this room where they met?" asked the magistrate. "Was she not concerned about going to such a place?"

I considered. "I think the lure of the meeting overcame any scruples. She had been there before; she seemed familiar with the arrangements."

"But it was a brothel," protested the magistrate.

I shrugged. "It is not my district, so I cannot be certain, but that is what the school caretaker said. It seems the hole in the wall was discovered by accident, and he started watching the whores and their gentleman friends." The magistrate raised an eyebrow but said nothing. "Then Buxton took over the room for his meetings; perhaps the abbess owed him a favour. Keane – our snitch – was on an errand to the room one day and spotted the peeping caretaker. He now bribes the caretaker to let him take his turn at the spy hole when Buxton is in residence – an insurance policy, if you will. He reasoned that the more he knew about Buxton, the safer he was. Until Charlie Gordon was killed, and Sophy."

"And now it's too rich for his blood, and he's offering to betray his former friends in exchange for his own skin," said Conant.

I nodded. "That's about it."

"Make sure that he does, Sam," said the magistrate. "Were it not for you, I would be hauling in this Francis Buxton for questioning right now."

"But who would speak against him, sir?" I asked. "Anyone who works with him will be frightened, and those who attend his special meetings will be ashamed. I cannot imagine our lady of quality standing before the court and telling the world that she visited the back room of a brothel in North Street."

Conant gave me a tight smile. "Indeed," he said. "But we must move soon, Sam, or I will have to answer for it."

CHAPTER THIRTY-ONE

In the physic garden

WEDNESDAY 5TH NOVEMBER 1828

Keane was waiting for us at the same table in the White Hart. This time, however, he had a battered carpet-bag at his feet, and he caught me looking at it.

"The West Country, sir, as we agreed," he said. He leaned forward. "Please, sir. I dare not stay any longer, after tonight."

The potboy reached over my shoulder to put three tankards on the table. Wilson waited until I had picked up mine before he lifted his and drank deeply; it had been a long walk to Shoreditch.

"Do as we ask this evening, Mr Keane," I said, "and I will keep my side of the bargain. Mr Wilson will walk with you to the Swan with Two Necks in Lad Lane, and there you can get the mail coach to Bath or Devizes or wherever you wish."

"The mail coach?" repeated Keane. "I'm no topping man, Mr Plank."

"Your ticket will be paid for, Mr Keane," I said, draining my tankard. "An outside seat only, mind you – but it's a sight quicker than walking. Now, let's get to business."

We had been waiting close to the wall alongside the vinegar yard for about twenty minutes when the wooden gate opened and people started leaving in small clusters, most of them talking excitedly.

"Must have been a good meeting," observed Keane.

We waited a few minutes more until a woman came out on her own and Keane nudged me. He whistled and she looked over. He beckoned to her.

"Eliza," he said in a loud whisper. "It's me: Tobias."

Eliza glanced back over her shoulder then pulled her shawl tight around her and walked towards us.

"What are you doing skulking out here, Toby?" she asked. She caught sight of Wilson and me and stopped. "And who are these two? More of Buxton's bullies?"

"Miss Eliza Mason?" I asked, stepping out of the shadow.

Eliza glanced from Keane to me, and nodded.

"My name is Constable Samuel Plank," I continued, "from Great Marlborough Street. I have been observing you for quite some time now, and I think you are a fraud." I watched her face carefully for a reaction, but she kept quiet and calm. "You convince people that you can intercede for them with their departed loved ones, and for this they pay you money."

"Or, seen another way," she said, "the bereaved come to me for reassurance and comfort, and show their gratitude by making a donation."

I shook my head. "Now you are confusing yourself with a priest, Miss Mason."

"And you, Constable Plank, are confusing yourself with a magistrate," she countered. "But as Toby here will tell you, I am simply a worker."

Keane reached out and touched her on the arm. "The game's up, Eliza. They know about the special meetings." He pointed to the bag at his feet. "You won't see me again after tonight. And you can save yourself, if you talk to them." A note of bitterness entered his voice. "You know he won't trouble himself to save you, when the time comes."

We all three waited while Eliza considered.

"Is Toby right?" she asked me. "If I tell you what I know, you'll let me go?"

"I cannot promise that, Miss Mason," I said. "But I can promise that I will tell the magistrates how helpful you have been. As you say, you are simply a worker – you are not the ringleader."

She made up her mind. “You seem an honest man, constable – you don’t make promises you cannot keep. And your honesty deserves mine in return.” She glanced over her shoulder back towards the vinegar yard. “But not here.”

We set off down City Road, the four of us. We passed Tabernacle Row and a few steps later Eliza stopped and said, “In here”.

“Have you done with me now, constable?” asked Keane, looking nervously around him and shifting his carpet bag from one hand to the other.

“You’re really off then, are you, Toby?” said Eliza. “Probably for the best.” She reached across and touched him on the arm. “Look after yourself. Going somewhere nice?”

“To the…” started Tobias.

“Yes, time for you to leave us, Mr Keane,” I interrupted quickly. There is no point in making a fresh start if you drag all your old acquaintances with you. “Constable Wilson will walk with you to the inn, and pay for your place on the coach.” I held out my hand and Keane looked surprised but shook it. “Good luck to you,” I said, and took his arm to draw him to one side, so that Eliza could not overhear us. “Once you have cleared the city tomorrow morning,” I continued, “Constable Wilson and I will spread the word that a body has been discovered by the side of the road near Hounslow, and will give your description. If Francis Buxton is concerned about your whereabouts, his spies will soon hear of this. They doubtless already know that you have family in the west, and will assume that you were waylaid and robbed while trying to reach them. You would be wise never to return to London."

Keane ducked his head. "Thank you, sir," he said, "but I have no wish to see this place again."

Wilson cleared his throat, and the two of them walked away.

Eliza led me into a garden in front of a neat building, with two floors of arched windows and a pillared porch.

"The City Road Chapel," Eliza said. "Mr Wesley lived here, and is buried in the garden behind it. Those pillars," she pointed at the four holding up the porch, "are ships' masts – given to Mr Wesley by the late King."

"Indeed," I said.

The surprise must have shown in my voice. "A woman can be curious about the world around her, constable," she said. "I have a good brain." She walked to a tree which had a small stone bench under it and indicated that I should sit with her. "I often come here, to think. It is a physic garden – Mr Wesley wrote a book about using herbs to cure illnesses, and he grew all of the herbs here to show how simple it was."

"I must bring Mrs Plank here," I said. "She has a great interest in such things."

"So you have experience of women who think," said Eliza, a note of amusement in her voice.

"I suspect that most women think a great deal," I replied. "And much of it will be more sensible than what passes for thoughts in men's heads." I paused for a few moments. "Now tell me about landing this bigger fish, Miss Mason."

"Francis Buxton," she said, not looking at me but gazing instead around the garden. "John's brother – his younger brother, although you'd not know it to look at them. Perhaps it's true what they say, about sin showing in the face." She stopped as though expecting me to reply, but I simply waited, my notebook open on my knee. "I met the Buxton brothers about three years ago, when I went to an outdoor gathering near my home – Oundle, in Northamptonshire. John had just come out of Newgate," she glanced at me and I nodded, "and wanted to breathe some fresh air again. His time in gaol had turned him into a fine preacher; he always could speak well, but three years living among desperate and rough men had taught him how they think and what matters to them, and how he could use words to rouse them."

"And Francis?" I asked.

Eliza all but snorted. "It is as though God gave all the goodness to one brother and, when it came to making the second, realised He had none left. Francis never sees a person without wondering how he can profit from them."

"But you seemed happy enough dealing with him in that back room, in the building on North Street," I said.

She looked sharply at me, eyes narrowed. "Have you been spying on me, Constable Plank?" she asked.

"I do what needs to be done, Miss Mason," I replied mildly. "As I say, you were not forced against your will, as far as I could see."

"There are many types of force, sir," she said, looking away again into the distance. "From the moment I met Francis, I knew he was bad. But he liked the look of me, and my preference was of no concern to him. A man like that will take what he wants." She turned to look at me. "And he took what he wanted."

"So why come with him to London?" I asked.

"I did not come to London with Francis," she replied. "I followed John. I hoped that his goodness – his bravery – would repair me. And he was happy to let me join their little group. But he did not want me as a man wants a woman. John Buxton loves only God." There was an understandable note of bitterness in her voice. "When Francis saw how things were, he offered me a way to stay close to John. And I took it." She looked down at her lap.

"Speaking to the dead?" I asked.

She nodded wordlessly.

"Tobias Keane told me what you did, you and Francis," I said. "How you tricked John into believing that you were talking to his late mother. And yet you say you loved him."

"I did love him – I do love him," she said. "I would follow him to the ends of the earth. But once the baby was showing, there was no hiding from John what had happened, and I knew that he would never want me after that. And the speaking to the dead – well, it was a way of keeping close to him. He took care of me, I think he even admired me. But Francis would not let it rest there; he wanted more money. And so the special meetings started." She watched my hand as I made notes. "But make sure you get it down right," she pointed at my notebook. "John knew nothing about those meetings. That was all Francis. Francis and me."

I reached into my pocket for a handkerchief, but she shook her head, sat more upright and looked away. When she thought I wasn't watching, she quickly rubbed the tears from her cheeks.

"What about the other heralds?" I asked.

"Like I said, Francis always wanted more money," she replied. "And once he saw how good I was at it, how I learned how to listen to the hints people drop, and how to deliver the messages they want to her, he made me teach it to others."

"Including Sophy Saunders?" I asked.

She nodded. "Poor Sophy," she said sadly. "Poor, foolish Sophy. She thought that pamphlet would save her, that people would take pity on her and save her, when all she did was write her own death warrant." She shook her head. "She didn't even have the wit to disguise her name in it."

"And what of John Buxton?" I asked. "Is he also writing his own obituary?"

"What do you mean?" asked Eliza sharply, looking at me.

"Mr Buxton has disappeared," I said. "Missed events that were advertised. Has something happened to him?"

She shook her head. "John is a man of conscience. The murders of that man..."

"Charlie Gordon," I said.

"Of Charlie Gordon and Sophy will have troubled him enormously," she continued. "He takes things to heart. He is almost certainly alone somewhere, praying for guidance and forgiveness."

"While we consider forgiveness, Miss Mason," I said, "what has happened to your baby?"

Eliza's shoulders sagged. "My little boy," she said gently. "He would have gone the way of the others, but the good Lord at last smiled on me." I wondered whether she was mocking me, but she sounded genuine. "A young girl came to one of the meetings, and we were told that she had recently lost a child. I asked around, and she was a good, Christian girl, nicely set up. When I was speaking for her at the meeting, an idea came to me – and I told her that another baby would soon be sent to her. After the meeting I suggested that I give her my baby, and she thought it was all coming true, what the message had told her, and she agreed. She has him now, my little boy. She will care for him because I cannot." She smiled softly and looked out across the garden. I left her with her memories for a few moments.

"Miss Mason," I said eventually, "you said that your little boy could have gone the way of the others. What others? What happened to them?"

"Francis Buxton is a cruel man, Constable Plank," Eliza replied. "And a clever one. He sees opportunities." She turned to look at me. "While you were waiting for me outside the vinegar yard, did you notice the building across the road?"

"The lying-in hospital?" I asked.

She smiled sadly. "Francis noticed it too. It is a place for respectable women – married women. But sometimes even respectable married women can stray, and if her husband refuses to accept the child… Perhaps they have not lain together for some time, or she has confessed to relations with another man." Eliza shrugged. "You would be surprised how many babies are not wanted, constable. Or perhaps, given your line of work, you would not. Francis came to know one of the nurses at the hospital –

a weak, greedy woman, by all accounts – and they cooked up a scheme. She would alert him to an unwanted baby, and he would arrange for that baby to be taken and given to parents who wanted a child but could not have one."

As she said those words I felt my heart contract with pain, but I said nothing.

"That is no crime," continued Eliza, "but of course Francis did not do this out of love and charity. The parents taking the child would be encouraged to make a donation – a large donation, in many cases – to the hospital, for various expenses."

"But the hospital saw none of the money," I suggested.

She nodded. "It was shared between them – Francis and the nurse." She turned to me again and looked me straight in the eye. "I was not going to sell my baby, Constable Plank. Babies should not be sold. They are not things. They should be given, and given with love and hope. I gave my baby. I did not sell him." She stabbed at my notebook with her finger. "You write that down, constable." And I did so.

All the way home I wrestled with my conscience, with my heart, and – if I am honest – with my own pain and cowardice. Eliza Mason's story had been horrifying and tragic in equal measure, and I was sorely tempted to spare myself the distress of telling it to Martha. Any woman hearing such a tale would be touched, but a woman who had longed for a child for years would feel a particularly sharp sting. But as soon as I saw my wife – the concern in her eyes and the warmth of her embrace – I knew that I was not strong enough to keep Eliza to myself, or to forgo the comfort that I knew Martha would offer.

After supper, we sat by the fire. Martha reached into the basket at her feet, selecting a shirt of mine for mending, and as she examined the tear in it, said to me, "Right then, Sam, out with it."

I gave her a weak smile. "There's no hiding anything from you, Mrs Plank," I said.

She raised an eyebrow at me as she snipped off a piece of thread and tied a knot in the end of it. "Indeed there is not, Constable Plank. And no more should you want to."

I told her everything, from our meeting with Tobias Keane in the White Hart to the moment I had taken my leave of Eliza Mason in the chapel garden. She listened in silence, mostly stitching carefully but occasionally glancing at me. When I had finished, I looked at her. She put down the shirt and held out her hand. I took it and squeezed it.

"At least now we know that George's mother does not want him back," she said. "Or at least that she knows that she must not take him back – I cannot imagine that a mother ever gives up wanting her child."

I leaned over and took the shirt from Martha's lap, putting it back into her basket, before taking Martha's other hand and pulling her onto my lap. I wrapped my arms around her and she leaned against me. Together we looked into the fire.

CHAPTER THIRTY-TWO

The treasure trove

THURSDAY 6TH NOVEMBER 1828

Wilson was already in the back office at Great Marlborough Street when I arrived the next morning. I turned from hanging my coat on the hook to catch him yawning widely.

"Late night?" I asked as I sat down.

He nodded. "I took Keane to the Swan in Lad Lane, but the Bristol coach leaves at half past seven every evening and we had missed it, and he didn't want to wait for another day. So we walked on to the Belle Sauvage."

"Ludgate Hill?" I asked.

"That's the one. There's a coach goes to Bath from there at half past six in the morning." Wilson yawned again. "I was going to leave him there, waiting in the Belle, but he was so nervous that I thought he might change his mind and just disappear. So I waited until I could see him onto the coach and have a quiet word with the driver. By which time it was gone six, and so I just came straight here."

"Well done, lad," I said. "That was the right thing to do." Despite his tiredness, Wilson smiled broadly and sat a little straighter in his chair. I reached into my pocket, pulled out a few coins and handed them to him. "You need to go home for a few hours. Not your home: mine. Tell Mrs Plank to let you sleep in the chair by the fire, and to wake you at three and send you back here. She won't have time to be waiting on you, mind, so stop off in the Irish place round the corner for a threepenny ordinary."

Once Wilson had plodded heavily down the steps into the street, I turned instead to the side staircase leading up to Mr Conant's rooms. I knocked on his door and he called me in. As usual, he was sitting at his table working his way through a pile of papers. He glanced up and then went back to his reading.

"Good morning, Sam," he said distractedly. "You catch me just in time: I have a full morning of hearings ahead of me."

I walked over to him. "Can you spare me ten minutes, sir?" I asked. "We have made considerable progress with the Charlie Gordon matter, but I would be reluctant to go further without your approval."

"Charlie Gordon?" asked the magistrate, his eyes still on the papers in front of him.

"The body found in Carnaby Market. Throat slit. Label around his neck," I explained.

Conant nodded. "Too much vinegar can split Planks," he said. He took off his spectacles and placed them on top of his papers, then turned his chair to face me. "Sit down, Sam. The hearings can wait."

I told him about my encounters with Keane, and everything that Eliza had revealed about Francis Buxton's crimes. He listened carefully, nodding from time to time.

"Francis Buxton is not a forgiving man, nor a compassionate one," I said. "But – and this is where I turn to you – he is a wealthy one. We know that Eliza was paid well when she visited fine houses, like the Palgraves'. Charlie Gordon said that collections after meetings at the vinegar yard could sometimes yield as much as two pounds. And as for the special meetings, well, we know that Josiah Welford was willing to hand over everything he and his wife had saved over decades. There must be a deal of money somewhere."

"And you have an idea where, I take it?" asked Conant. "And you want me to instruct you to visit those premises?"

"I would like to gain entry to the room I saw from the outbuilding in the school yard," I replied. "The front entrance will be on North Street, but I am as yet unsure of the exact number; I will need to pace it out."

Conant turned back to his desk, put on his spectacles and pulled a blank sheet of paper towards him. "I shall write it simply as North Street, and leave a space for you to fill in when you have the number of the premises," he said, dipping his pen. "Entry and arrest?" he asked as he wrote.

"If you would, sir," I replied.

He finished the warrant, signed it and dusted it with sand. Once it was dry he shook it clean and held it out. I walked to the table and took it from him.

"Constable Wilson will be going with you, I assume," he said. "I should not like you to confront this Buxton fellow on your own."

"All in hand, sir," I said. "All in hand."

Wilson looked like a new man when I met him the foot of the steps leading down from Oxford Street to Blenheim Street.

"You slept, then," I said as I led him back up the steps.

"I did," he replied. "I had the threepenny ordinary on my way home this morning, and when I woke Mrs Plank gave me a pot of tea and a slice of plum loaf. And she asked me to give you yours." He reached into his coat pocket and brought out a paper-wrapped package. I unwrapped it, broke off a corner of the cake and quickly put it into my mouth before wrapping it back up and sliding it into my own pocket. "Where to, then, sir?" asked Wilson, pointing to a crumb on my front.

"North Street," I said. "Near the vinegar yard. Francis Buxton's place of business."

"That's quite a step," said Wilson.

"Just as well we're taking a coach, then," I said, raising my arm to catch the attention of a passing jarvey. He pulled his animals to a halt and we climbed in after giving him our destination. In truth I had been intending to walk, but in a coach a man can concentrate more fully on enjoying a slice of plum loaf.

Half an hour later, Wilson and I were standing outside the school in Tabernacle Row. I banged on the door, and once again it was opened the smallest amount while the caretaker lifted his lantern and took stock of his visitors.

"Constable Samuel Plank and Constable William Wilson of Great Marlborough Street," I said. "We were here a week ago with Tobias Keane." The caretaker hesitated. "We have no interest in your and your small purses, old man," I said. "All we want from you is information. The number of the house on North Street – the one whose room we saw into. Tell us that and you can go back to your fireside."

The caretaker whispered something and I leaned forward. "Number seven," he said again, and shut the door firmly in my face.

We walked back out onto City Road and turned into North Street. The tall houses crowded together on either side, staring at each other across the narrow lane. Number seven was in the second block, with a narrow passageway alongside it; this, I surmised, was how Buxton and his cronies would go in and out, unobserved by the occupants. Armed with our warrant, however, Wilson and I could go right through the front door, on which I knocked with authority. After a few moments I heard a window scraping open above our heads, and I took hold of Wilson's arm to pull him out of the way in case something unwelcome was thrown down onto us. In the event, a woman simply looked out and then went back in, banging the window shut again. I could hear shouting inside the house, and after a minute or two more the front door was opened by a grubby little maid of about fourteen. She wore a dress that was too big for her, and the lace cap jammed on her head was comical in its large size and considerable filth.

"Yes?" she asked unwelcomingly.

I held the warrant in front of her face and she looked at it with mild curiosity.

"My name is Constable Samuel Plank," I said, "acting on the instructions of John Conant Esquire, magistrate." The maid's eyes grew bigger with every word. "This is a warrant – an order – from the magistrate which permits Constable Wilson and me to come into this house and look around." I leaned forward just as the maid tried to shut the door and put out my hand to block it. "We'll wait in the hallway, girl – go and fetch your mistress."

The maid scurried off and Wilson and I stepped into the hallway, closing the door behind us. It was a dark, dank space, with the smell of a building that is seldom, if ever, aired. Over our heads we could hear urgent footsteps, the dragging of furniture and the slamming of doors.

"Hiding equipment," I observed to Wilson. "And possibly customers."

Finally the door to the front room opened and a rather large woman came out. She was taller than I, and about as broad, and – as much as it was possible to discern in the dim light – in need of a shave.

"Gentlemen," she said in a fluting voice, "such an honour for my little house. Please, do come into my parlour." She stood back to let us pass and we walked into a room which, as Martha would have observed, needed a good flick of the duster. "Please," she said again, indicating an overfilled sofa. I sat down, but Wilson took up his usual post, standing with his back to the door. The woman looked a little uneasy at this, but decided to make the best of it by smiling sweetly. She sat in an armchair opposite me, carefully arranging her skirts as she did so. "Millie tells me that you have a rather alarming piece of paper with you," she said.

I handed her the warrant. "As you can see, Mrs…" I started.

"Bennett," she said. "Mrs Susanna Bennett." She looked down at the paper.

"As you can see, Mrs Bennett, it is a warrant from a magistrate in Great Marlborough Street, tasking us with entering this house and searching it, and giving us the power to arrest anyone whom we suspect of committing a crime."

"A crime? Goodness!" twittered Mrs Bennett, using the warrant to fan herself.

I held out my hand for the warrant and she returned it. "Mrs Bennett," I said seriously, "Constable Wilson and I care not one jot what you are hiding beneath those skirts. We are not here to shut down your molly house. Our concern is with the activities that go on in one of your back rooms – activities involving Mr Francis Buxton." I watched her carefully and I saw fear flash into her eyes. "And this warrant means that you have no choice, Mrs Bennett: if you do not permit us to execute the warrant, we will arrest you. And when they hear of your refusal, the magistrates might well be rather more interested in your unusual services than we are." I stood and put the folded warrant into my coat pocket. "Now, Mrs Bennett, that back room if you please."

The abbess led us out of her parlour and down the hallway past several closed doors. The air did not become any fresher, and from behind one of the doors we heard a low male voice and then a woman warning him to be quiet. At the end of the hallway was another closed door; Mrs Bennett reached for the bunch of keys hanging from her waist and rapped on the door. When there was no answer, she unlocked it and stood aside to let us past. I shook my head.

"Ladies first," I said. If someone was waiting behind the door with a cudgel, I felt sure our stately hostess would withstand the blow better than I. Mrs Bennett walked into the room, twisting her hands nervously, and Wilson and I followed her. I looked around. It was as I had seen from the spy hole in the wall, but what I had not been able to see from that limited vantage point was a door leading to the side alleyway, and a large, deep, dark wooden cupboard running the length of the back wall, to about chest height.

"What's that?" I asked, pointing at it.

"Buxton had that built when he, well, when he took the room for himself," said Mrs Bennett, allowing her voice to drop to something closer to its natural pitch. "Brought in his own carpenter and materials."

"Have you never asked what is inside?" I asked.

"Have you met Francis Buxton?" she asked. I shook my head. "When you do, you will learn that he is not a man who likes to be bothered with questions."

I bent down to look at the cupboard. Each pair of doors – there were three pairs – had its own lock. "Do you have the keys to these?" I asked, knowing the answer.

"Of course not," said Mrs Bennett.

"In that case," I instructed, looking over my shoulder at her, "go to your kitchen and fetch us a knife – a strong one – and a piece of wood to put force on it." Mrs Bennett did not move. "The warrant, madam," I reminded her. "To search the premises and anything we find on them."

Mrs Bennett huffed with annoyance and left the room in a rustle of skirts.

"What do you expect to find in there?" asked Wilson, jerking his chin towards the cupboard.

I straightened up and stretched my back. "Money," I suggested. "Jewels. Small things of great value. Buxton is not a London man; he has not bought a property here. He is used to life on the road, and knows that sooner or later word of his frauds will reach the ears of the magistrates. A man like that will keep his assets in portable form, ready to make good his escape at any time. Thanks to Mr Keane, we may just be one step ahead of him."

Mrs Bennett came back into the room and held out to me the knife and a block of wood about the size of a brick.

I shook my head and pointed to Wilson. He took them from her and knelt down in front of the first cupboard.

"Should I try to save the lock?" he asked me.

"No," I said. "Buxton will know soon enough that we have been here. But put this across it before you put the knife in, in case of splinters." I handed him a scrap of cloth that I had found on the bed.

Wilson nodded, covered the lock with the cloth, felt the shapes with his fingertips and then inserted the point of the knife into the lock. With the block of wood he gave the end of the knife's handle a sharp whack. He lifted the cloth away and tried the cupboard door; it opened.

"Thank you, Mrs Bennett," I said, turning to her. "Go back to your parlour. I will come and see you when we have finished."

The abbess nodded tightly and left. I knelt down beside Wilson. He opened the cupboard door fully and we looked inside.

"He's tidy, I'll say that for him," observed Wilson.

And indeed he was. The cupboard was divided by three shelves, and its contents were sorted neatly by shelf. Piled up on the top shelf were leather purses tied with cords. I lifted one out; it was heavy so I untied the cord and dipped my hand into it – it was full of coins. On the middle shelf was a stack of small wooden boxes, like miniature chests. Wilson took one of these and opened it.

"Like the treasures of Aladdin," he said softly. "In that book of Arabian stories. Mrs Plank read it to little Martha and the other children, at the Blue Boar."

Knowing what pride I took in having taught Martha to read, and what pleasure she in her turn now took from books, Mr Conant was very generous in allowing me to borrow from his personal library. And I could remember him recommending Scott's "Arabian Nights Entertainments". How Martha's eyes had widened as we explored those distant lands together, and I smiled to think of Wilson sitting at her knee, like a little boy, listening to her read them aloud.

"Indeed," I said, looking at the sparkle and glint of the jewels in the box. "And what is on the lowest shelf?"

We both crouched down further to peer into the cupboard, and that is the last I remember for quite some time.

When I awoke my head was banging like a drum. I was sitting on the floor, leaning against the bed, with my legs stretched out and my hands tied in front of me. Wilson was next to me, in similar circumstances, and I nudged him. He groaned and lifted his head. I could see a trail of dried blood on his cheek.

"What happened?" he said thickly.

"We were hit from behind while we were looking into that cupboard," I said.

"Who?" he asked, looking slowly around the room.

I tried to shrug but it hurt my arms. "Mrs Bennett and one of her mollies, I should imagine," I said. "You know she is really a..."

"A man?" said Wilson. "Of course. I'm not blind."

"And a man who is more frightened of Francis Buxton than of the magistrates," I observed. "No doubt she means to serve us up to him when he returns, to show her loyalty."

"In that case," said Wilson, shaking his head to clear it, "we had best get ourselves free."

He had just hauled himself to his knees when we heard a key in a lock. We looked towards the door leading to the house, but realised that it was coming from the other door – the entrance from the side passage. Buxton. Wilson looked at me with wide eyes.

The door opened, but rather than Buxton it was Eliza. She stopped when she saw us, me on the floor and Wilson on his knees as if in prayer, and then quickly came into the room and shut the door behind her.

"You, she said, pointing at Wilson, "sit back down as you were." Wilson looked at me and I nodded, so he did as he was told.

Eliza strode across the room to the other door, opened it and yelled down the corridor for Mrs Bennett. We heard footsteps and that good lady arrived; Eliza pulled her into the room and shut the door.

"What is all this?" she asked angrily, waving her arm at us. "What have you done?"

Mrs Bennett looked confused. "I thought Francis... I thought it is what he would want."

Eliza drew herself up and put her hands on her hips. She was a good foot shorter than Mrs Bennett, but the larger woman cowered.

"Francis Buxton," said Eliza, "is not the be all and end all. These," she waved at us again, "are constables, Mrs Bennett. Magistrates' constables. Sent here on official business. Magistrates do not expect their constables to be beaten and tied. Magistrates can send you to the Old Bailey, and the judge at the Old Bailey can send you to the gallows."

With each phrase Mrs Bennett grew paler. She looked down at me, and I did my best, given my ludicrous position, to look as stern as possible.

Eliza continued. "However, I am sure that these two gentlemen can understand why you did what you did." Wilson opened his mouth to say something but I glared at him and he shut it. Eliza went on. "If you free them immediately and summon a coach to take them home, perhaps we can persuade them to forget what has happened here today. And there will be no need to involve Mr Buxton, who is on his way. Would that be possible, Constable Plank?"

She looked down at me. The warning she was giving was clear: if Buxton found us here, he would not stop at tying us up. If we needed any proof of how he dealt with people who crossed him, we had only to remember Charlie Gordon and Sophy Saunders.

"That seems a very sensible proposal, Miss Mason," I said.

Martha took one look at us and stood to one side to let us into the kitchen.

"Coats off, wash your hands, and sit down, both of you," she said. We did as we were told, and after busying herself at the stove she put a bowl of broth and a large wedge of bread in front of each of us. Wilson fell on his like a starving man. I was more concerned about Martha and I looked at her; she smiled sadly and pointed at my bowl, so I ate to please her.

When we had finished, Martha cleared the dishes and put a bowl of warm water on the table. With a cloth and a little dab of soft soap, she cleaned first Wilson and then me. As she did so, she commented on our injuries.

"Just a small cut on the back of your head, William – less than half an inch long, but head cuts do bleed." She went to a cupboard and took out a small pot. She took off its lid, sniffed the contents, and then dabbed a little on

Wilson's cut. He winced. "Yarrow ointment," said Martha. "To aid healing. I will give you some to take home, and your mother can reapply it. All done."

"Thank you, Mrs Plank," said Wilson. He made to stand but Martha gave him a look and he sat down again.

"Rest a while, William," she said. "I'll see to Sam, and then there's a bread pudding you can share." She turned her attention to me, running her hands over my head and noting when I flinched. "No broken skin for you, Sam – you're a tough old bird. Although you'd think you might have learned from that incident in the coach maker's a couple of years ago, not to go ferreting in places where someone can creep up on you. Try and remember next time, if there's any working memory left in your noggin." She sighed theatrically. "You'll both have a headache for a while yet. Do you know who hit you?"

"We can't be certain," I said, "but we think it was a man in a dress."

"Well, it takes all sorts," said Martha, putting a dish of pudding in front of each of us. I didn't ask whether she was referring to us or to Mrs Bennett.

CHAPTER THIRTY-THREE

An invitation

FRIDAY 7TH NOVEMBER 1828

Martha was right: when I woke the next morning, the headache was terrible. I felt gingerly on the back of my skull, and a lump about the size of a shilling was tender to the touch. I slowly lifted my head from the pillow and then sat on the edge of the bed for a moment.

Martha called up the stairs. "Time to be up, Sam. Breakfast is ready, and there's a message been delivered."

"The perilous pond?" asked Mr Conant, raising en eyebrow. "It sounds like the very worst kind of novel."

I smiled. "It does, yes. It was called that for centuries, thanks to the number of people who drowned there. The current owner prefers the more enticing 'Peerless Pool'."

"An outdoor bathing pool, you say?" asked the magistrate.

I nodded. "Very popular in the summer, and used regularly by bluecoat boys."

"And why do you think this Eliza Mason is requesting that you attend a meeting there this evening?" asked Conant.

I had already told him the outcome of our visit the previous day to North Street.

"I think she is looking for a way to escape from Francis Buxton," I said. "She knows that Mrs Bennett will eventually tell him the truth about what happened at North Street; Eliza's tale about disturbing burglars in the back room does not show the abbess in a good light, and she is a weak and cowardly woman who will do all she can to save her own skin. And once Buxton knows, he will come after us – Constable Wilson and me – and after Eliza for allowing us to leave."

"But why does she not just flee?" asked the magistrate.

"Ah, I have been mulling that myself," I said. "And I think there are two reasons. First, you see she says in her note that 'John knows all and forgives all'?" Conant nodded. "Eliza told me when we spoke in the physic garden that she loves John Buxton. And I assume she means me to understand that she has confessed everything to him: that she was only pretending to speak to the dead, and that she tricked him and many others, but that Francis made her do it. And, being a godly fellow, John Buxton has forgiven her. Perhaps she harbours hopes of making a life with him, and so she chooses to stay. And second, well, I think this is the more important." I leaned forward. "Eliza is whip-smart, sir. She knows that if she runs, she will spend the rest of her life looking behind her for Francis Buxton or one of his cronies. She needs to be rid of him properly. And, as her note says, if we attend the meeting at the perilous pond tonight, we will see all we need to be able to put Francis before the judge."

Conant frowned. "I am uneasy about sending you there with just Constable Wilson. He is a brave lad, but if this Francis Buxton is cornered – he has already shown himself capable of murder."

"It is a public meeting, sir," I said. "Called by John Buxton, not by Francis. Not one of the special meetings in private. Francis Buxton would be foolish to attempt to harm us with so many witnesses – and he is not a foolish man."

"Far from it," said the magistrate grimly. "Far from it."

CHAPTER THIRTY-FOUR

The bathing pool

WEDNESDAY 12TH NOVEMBER 1828

As Wilson and I rattled along in the coach, he pulled the collar of his coat around his neck.

"It's a chilly evening," I observed, "but better than the fog we had yesterday."

"Aye," he replied. "Do these Methodists meet outside all year round, in all weathers?"

"I think so," I said. "They believe it brings them closer to God. And it allows them to preach in their own way, rather than fitting in with the established church. But it's not a service we're going to; according to Eliza's note, this is one of Buxton's meetings, like the ones in the vinegar yard."

Wilson rubbed his hands together and blew on them. "So why not hold it in the vinegar yard then, in the warm?" he asked.

"I have been wondering that," I replied. "And it seems to me that the water might be important – the bathing pool. Perhaps a baptism or some other cleansing ceremony."

Wilson shivered. "Well, if they think to tempt me into that pool in this weather, they are going to be disappointed."

As directed, when we reached the junction of Old Street Road and City Road the jarvey turned left and then stopped his coach at the entrance to Baldwin Street. Wilson and I climbed out and I reached up to hand some coins to the jarvey.

"Will we find another coach in about an hour?" I asked.

Swaddled in a dark cloak, its collar turned up and his hat pulled down low, the jarvey shrugged. "You might and you might not," he growled. "For a small consideration, sir, I'll tie up me beasts and take a jar in the Old Fountain Knights, just along there, and wait for you." With his whip he indicated Baldwin Street.

"You do that," I said. "Half now and half later." I reached up and handed him another coin.

The jarvey nodded and urged his horses forward. Wilson and I walked into Baldwin Street and joined the small crowd of people – perhaps twenty of us – heading in the same direction. We turned left into Bath Row and slowed as we passed one by one through the gate into the little park surrounding the bathing pool. Lanterns had been placed around to light the scene – some on the low wall surrounding the pool and some hanging from the trees – and there was an air of anticipation and excitement among our fellow guests.

"It's bigger than I thought," said Wilson. "What's that – nearly two hundred feet long and a hundred feet wide?"

"Have you never been here?" I asked. He shook his head. "I came here a few times as a lad," I said. "Not as a paying visitor, mind you: we used to climb over the wall and then bolt if the keeper saw us. It's not that deep – about five foot at the deepest – and very refreshing on a hot day. In the winter it turns into an ice rink."

"It's not far off that this evening," said Wilson, pursing his lips and blowing out a cloud of breath. "See: perishing." He stopped and peered into the distance. "Over there, sir – John Buxton."

I followed his gaze. Perhaps feeling our eyes upon him, the preacher glanced over at us and raised a hand in greeting. He walked over to us. As before, he was dressed in plain, dark clothes, with the addition of a simple wooden cross hanging on a long cord around his neck.

"Gentlemen," he said warmly, shaking each of us by the hand in turn. "I am delighted to see you here."

"We are pleased to attend," I replied, " and grateful to Miss Mason for inviting us. We were concerned for your wellbeing, Mr Buxton."

"And why should that be?" he asked.

I explained about the complaints that had been made to John Conant about cancelled events.

"Ah yes, I am sorry to have caused concern and inconvenience," he said. "Please pass on my apologies to Mr Conant. The truth of the matter is that my spiritual life was being neglected. The meetings – the heralds – are all important, of course, but if I am not spiritually fulfilled myself, I cannot help others. And so I took myself out of the city for a while, and returned to what I know best: preaching on the road."

"Indeed," I said. "But you are spiritually fulfilled now?"

Buxton smiled broadly. "I am, constable. And very much looking forward to this evening, which is a very important one for my family." He looked past us and then waved his arm vigorously to call someone over. "This is my brother Francis."

Wilson and I both turned to greet the newcomer. Like his brother, Francis wore dark trousers and plain boots, but his upper half was encased in a white smock, rather like a priest's surplice, falling to just above his knees. He held out his hand and I shook it.

"Francis," said John, putting a hand on his brother's shoulder, "may I introduce you to Constable Sam Plank and Constable William Wilson."

Francis's eyes narrowed slightly but his smile did not falter. "Gentlemen, it is a pleasure to meet you," he said.

Just then the majestic bell of St Luke's started tolling the hour, and people moved towards the northern end of the pool, where marble steps led down into the water. The Buxton brothers said farewell to us and walked away together. They took up their positions at the top of the marble steps, and Eliza Mason appeared and stood with them so that she and John were flanking Francis. John raised both his arms and started to speak.

"Brothers and sisters," he said in his warm, clear tones, "I welcome you here this evening, and thank you for braving the cold to witness this joyful ceremony." He dropped his arms and took hold of Francis's hand. "This is my brother Francis. For many years, through pride and anger, we have been estranged."

A woman standing near us shook her head sorrowfully.

The preacher continued. "He injured me, but I then compounded that injury. I did not turn the other cheek, I did not reach out to him. Instead, I turned my back on him. We did not care for each other as brothers – as godly men – should care for each other, and this hurt many people around us, including our beloved mother, who went to her grave praying for our reconciliation. And last week Francis came to me and he asked my forgiveness. And I asked his. And now we are once again brothers in the eyes of God." He turned to Francis and the two men embraced. "And to mark his return to the path of righteousness, Francis has asked to be cleansed by baptism, following the example shown to us by Jesus in the Bible."

John took off his coat and handed it to Eliza, who folded it over her arm. The brothers both bent and unlaced their boots and removed them. Then John held out his hand to Francis, and they stepped together into the water. They descended the steps until they were both submerged up to the waist, and then Francis tipped backwards until he was lying in the pool. John put his hands on his brother's shoulders.

"Dear Lord," he called out, "please take unto your heart this thy child Francis, and cleanse him of his sins. In the name of the Father." He gently pushed Francis under the water and then allowed him to rise out of it. "And of the Son," he said as he pushed him in again and then allowed him to rise. "And of the Holy Spirit." This time he held him under for a few seconds longer and then lifted him once more. He bent over his brother and spoke to him, and then looked over his shoulder at Eliza. Then he grabbed at Francis's body, his hands scrabbling to get a grip on the white material. Eliza dropped the coat she was holding and splashed into the pool, her dark skirt billowing around her as she stumbled down the steps. Together they pulled Francis to the edge of the pool and two men stepped forward and helped them haul him out of the water. They laid him on the side of the pool and someone rushed up with a set of bellows, just like the ones we had seen in the receiving house in Green Park.

Wilson and I walked quickly to the little group now surrounding the body; Eliza held the tip of the bellows in Francis's mouth while one of the men pumped them. John was kneeling on the ground, crouched over his brother, and frantically rubbing his chest to warm him and to stimulate breathing. But there was no response to any of it, and the corpse's lips were already turning blue.

I leaned down and put a hand on John's shoulder. He stopped his feverish movement and sat back on his heels.

"I am to blame," he said, his voice breaking. "Francis had a weak heart, and the water is so cold. I should have stopped him. When he suggested the baptism – I should have stopped him."

Eliza looked up from wringing out her skirts. "You could not have stopped him, John," she said fiercely. "He was determined. No-one could ever stop Francis when he was determined."

The crowd stood around us in silent shock.

"Go and find that jarvey," I said to Wilson. "In the tavern. Tell him to bring the coach to the end of the street, and he can take the body to the coroner."

By the time I reached home, it was near midnight and there was a frost settling. I tiptoed in quietly, thinking Martha to be in bed, but there was a faint glow coming from the sitting room and there she was, dozing in her chair, with a shawl around her shoulders and her darning unfinished on her knee. I woke her gently and suggested going straight to bed but she took hold of my chilled hand and felt my cold face, and led me instead into the kitchen. Ten minutes later we were sitting at the table with a cup of hot chocolate in front of each of us, and I told her what had happened that evening.

"Poor Mr Buxton," she said, shaking her head. "What a terrible loss, just as he and his brother had resolved their differences." She shuddered as a thought crossed her mind. "I am thankful that I was not there. I might have gone, a few weeks ago. But I certainly should not like to see a man drown." She reached over and patted my hand. "I know that you are made of sterner stuff, Sam, but still, I am sorry for you." Martha stood and cleared our cups, putting them on the side to be seen to in the morning. "Did Eliza give you the information that she promised?" she asked. "About Francis Buxton's crimes? Before the death, I mean. Not that you can use it now, of course."

CHAPTER THIRTY-FIVE

The coroner's report

THURSDAY 13TH NOVEMBER 1828

Martha's question was still bothering me the next day as I went about my business. First thing in the morning I called on Mr Conant to tell him what had happened at the gathering the previous evening; he was relieved to hear that John Buxton had reappeared, but sorry to learn of his brother's death. Like me, he was always happier when a criminal faced justice rather than cheated it by death.

I had told Tom Neale that we were expecting a report from the coroner and that he should keep it to one side for me, rather than handing it to another constable. It was nearly five o'clock when I returned from a hard afternoon of searching for men who did not want to be found and Martha's pigeon pie was on my mind. When she had promised it at breakfast, my heart had lifted: it was one of my favourite meals, and a signal that the worst of our estrangement was over.

Tom looked up from his counter as I walked in.

"It arrived about an hour ago," he said, pointing to a letter. "From the coroner." He watched as I broke the seal and unfolded the paper. "As you expected?"

I shook my head. "Far from it," I said. "Is he in?" I pointed to the ceiling.

"I believe so," said Tom. "Out to dinner later, so he might be dressing. Do you want me to call Thin Billy?"

"No need," I said, tucking the report into my pocket. "I'll go up myself."

I knocked on the door of Conant's dining room. There was no reply so I knocked again, more loudly; as Tom had guessed, he was probably in his dressing room and could not hear me. I went in and called out.

"I'll be with you in a moment, Sam," replied the magistrate. And indeed he appeared almost immediately, running a finger around his collar and jutting out his chin. "Whoever decided that men should wear collars like dogs should be horse-whipped," he said. "We'll have to be quick, I'm afraid: I am accompanying Lily to the opera this evening, and although I would be delighted to miss one or two hours of the wretched thing, she does like to be prompt."

I smiled; Conant could protest as much as he wanted, but we all knew how proud he was to be seen with his beautiful daughter on his arm.

"I just wanted to show you this," I said, handing him the paper. "The coroner's report on Francis Buxton."

Conant walked to the table and picked up his spectacles, pinching them onto his nose before reading the report. He looked up at me with surprise.

"Not angina pectoris, then?" he said. "I thought you said it was a seizure brought on by the cold water."

"We all did," I said. "It made sense, and that's how it appeared."

"Well, you know what they say about appearances," said Conant, handing the paper back to me.

CHAPTER THIRTY-SIX

From Addison to Bennet

FRIDAY 14TH NOVEMBER 1828

"Stiletto?" asked Wilson as we walked briskly down Great Titchfield Street, on our way to hail a coach on Oxford Street. Given the urgency of the matter, Conant had approved the expenditure. "What sort of a word is that? Foreign?"

"Italian," I replied. "From the Latin word *stilus,* which was the long, pointed writing instrument they used in Roman times. And so a stiletto blade is very long and thin." I gestured with my hands.

"And that's what the coroner says killed Francis Buxton?" asked Wilson.

"He found a puncture wound in his back, going right through to his heart," I replied.

We stepped out onto Oxford Street and looked around. A coach had just ambled past, heading west, so I raised my arm and called out. The jarvey turned to look at me and I pointed in the opposite direction. He raised his whip to indicate that he had understood, and turned his animals into John Street. He went around Oxford Market and appeared behind us. I told him our destination and we climbed in while he waited for a gap in the flow of carts heading towards the city.

Wilson settled back into the seat. "But if there was a stab wound," he said, "why did we not see any blood? I helped lift the body into the coach, and there was nothing."

"In very cold water," I explained, "the movement of the blood is slowed down. It's the same in cold air – you know how your hands and feet feel chilled in winter?" Wilson nodded. "That's because the blood is sluggish," I continued. "And this means that you don't bleed as much. And it was a very small wound – very small, but very precise. And he was wearing several layers of clothes, wasn't he?" Wilson nodded again. "They would have soaked up what blood there was. And of course no-one was looking at his back."

"But we were there," protested Wilson. "We watched it all. Francis was obviously perfectly well when we met him, and when he stepped into the water, so it must have happened during the baptism. And the preacher held his hands up high before he started – there was no knife to be seen."

The coach jolted over a rough patch of road and we both reached for the straps to keep steady.

"Think carefully," I said. "Think carefully about what we saw. Go over it all again in your mind. Close your eyes if it helps." Wilson looked at me in surprise. "Go on," I said.

He closed his eyes and I waited. Perhaps three minutes passed. He opened his eyes suddenly and looked at me. "Eliza," he said.

I nodded.

The large wooden gates of the vinegar yard were standing open, and four wagons were lined up inside, being loaded with barrels. I walked up to the man who seemed to be overseeing the loading and asked to be directed to the office; he looked at my uniform and pointed wordlessly to a wooden staircase in the corner. Wilson stayed in the yard and I walked up the stairs. I knocked on the door and went into a large room that stretched the length of the yard, with large windows looking down into it, so that anyone working in the office could see everything that was happening in the yard below.

There was a young lad bent over a desk near the door and I asked him where I could find the man in charge, and he pointed to the other end of the room, to a panel with a door in it. I crossed the office, past another dozen or so men writing in ledgers, adding up figures, reading through papers and the like, and knocked on the door, on which was written in gold lettering 'Wm Addison, Esq. – Manager'.

"Come," said a voice inside, and I went in. Sitting behind a desk was a neat fellow of about sixty, with grey hair and well-tended whiskers. He did not look up immediately, as he was writing, but when he did he saw what I was and jumped to his feet.

"Constable," he said. "Is there a problem with one of our carts, or our men?" He glanced down into the yard and no doubt spotted Wilson standing sentry near the gate. "Do you have a warrant of some sort?" He suddenly grasped the edge of his desk. "Not for me, sir?"

"No, sir, nothing of the sort," I said. "Shall we?" I indicated the seat on my side of the desk and he nodded. We both sat down. "I am Constable Samuel Plank, of Great Marlborough Street, acting on the instructions of the magistrate John Conant." Addison nodded. "And I am interested in trying to find Mr John Buxton."

Addison's face relaxed and he sat back in his seat. "Ah, John," he said. "The preacher." I nodded. "Well, today is…" he looked down at the almanac on his desk, "yes, today is Thursday, so we do not expect him today. His meetings are held on Wednesday evenings."

"So you know of his meetings?" I asked.

"Of course," said the manager with some surprise. "Nothing happens in this yard without my knowing, constable."

"And you know what happens at those meetings?" I asked.

"I do," said Addison. "I have attended them myself, and Mr Buxton uses these premises at my invitation."

"Has he used them recently?" I asked.

"I can tell you exactly when he held his meetings," said Addison, and starting turning the pages of his almanac. "Every Wednesday, for several months now, except..." he turned a page back and then forward again, "except recently." He turned the almanac on the desk so that I could read it, and pointed to the relevant entries. "Here, you can see – my clerk fills this in for me, so that we have a record of everything. John Buxton was here on Wednesday 8th October, and then again on Wednesday 15th October, just as usual, and then there is a gap. And that's one, two, three Wednesdays that he missed."

"Plus yesterday," I said.

Addison looked up at me. "Oh, is that why you are here? One of the lads told me this morning; Mr Buxton held a special gathering yesterday evening, just around the corner at the bathing pool. And what a tragedy," the manager leaned towards me conspiratorially, "his brother died in his arms."

"It is indeed a tragedy," I said. "I would like to express my condolences to Mr Buxton, if I can. Do you happen to know his address?"

Addison shook his head. "Sadly, no," he said. "Mr Buxton does not maintain a household in London; he prefers to stay with friends, so that he is free to return to the road when he feels the spiritual call. He once stayed a fortnight with me and my family, and very welcome he was too. Mr Buxton has no shortage of friends happy to accommodate him – he is such a good and decent man." He sighed deeply. "With this grief, I should not be surprised if he has taken himself off to seek spiritual strength and replenishment."

"Nor I, sir," I said.

Wilson looked expectantly at me as I walked across the yard to him and I shook my head.

"North Street, then," he said.

Two minutes later he was banging on the door of number seven.

"I doubt they get many visitors at this hour," I said, and indeed the curtains of Mrs Bennett's parlour were still firmly closed against the light. "Knock again – louder," I instructed, and Wilson did as he was told, the noise setting off a few dogs in the surrounding streets. After about five minutes we heard bolts being scraped back, and the door was hauled open by the maid, wearing the same dress that all but swallowed her up, but missing her cap. Before she could say anything, Wilson stepped forward and pushed past her into the hallway. She cowered and I took pity on her.

"You're not in trouble, girl," I said. "You remember us – the constables." She nodded. "Go and get Mrs Bennett, and tell her we're waiting in the parlour."

The maid scampered off and Wilson and I returned to the dusty parlour. He looked around with distaste, and walked across to the window to open the curtains. Light poured into the room and did nothing to improve it. The door opened and in came the mistress of the house, screwing up her eyes against the brightness. The shadow of her beard was even more pronounced this time, and I guessed that we had called on her before her morning ablutions.

"Constables," she said. "Another delightful surprise."

"You will forgive me, Mrs Bennett, if I am not as delighted as you are," I said. "I still have the lump on my head from your last welcome."

The abbess said nothing, simply smoothing down her skirt and then putting a tidying hand to her wig.

"As you obviously rise rather late in this establishment," I continued, "word may not have reached you about the events of yesterday evening." Mrs Bennett raised a questioning eyebrow. "Francis Buxton was murdered," I said.

"Murdered?" she echoed, forgetting in her surprise to maintain what she obviously took for a refined female voice.

"Murdered," I repeated. "Not far from here – at the bathing pool."

"Who did it?" she asked. I looked at Wilson and shook my head.

"We would like to take another look at that back room," I said. I watched her carefully and there it was, as clear as could be: the glint of greed in her eyes.

"Surely you are busy men, constables, with a murderer roaming the streets," she said, giving a mock shudder. "You should not have to waste your time acting as porters. Allow me to assist you: I will pack up all that is left in that room and send it on to you at, where was it, Great Marlborough Street."

"I think not, Mrs Bennett," I said. "Now, if you please: the back room."

As we had done before, we followed the abbess down the corridor, past several closed doors. But this time, once Mrs Bennett had unlocked the door of the room, I pushed past her and went in first. All the doors of the cupboard against the far wall were standing open. And I could see immediately that every shelf was empty. Mrs Bennett walked in behind me.

"The whoreson's taken the lot," she hissed.

I could not have put it better myself.

CHAPTER THIRTY-SEVEN

A parcel for Alice

WEDNESDAY 19TH NOVEMBER 1828

Wilson and I were walking home in the dark, our thoughts turning to supper. I had sensed all day that there was something troubling him, but I knew better than to force the matter. Wilson was a man of few words, and prising them out of him rarely worked; he would talk when he was ready. And he was ready when we had just crossed Foley Street.

"I saw Alice on Sunday," he said. "At the Blue Boar. Her and the baby – little George."

"Aye," I said.

"And I told her about Buxton's tricks," he continued. "Carefully, like. Not all in a rush. I explained it to her, how he did it, and about Eliza's part in it."

"Was she upset?" I asked as we turned left into Clipstone Street. I could have stopped, but men often find it easier to talk side by side than face to face.

"Not as much as I feared she might be," he admitted. And now he did stop and put his hand on my arm to halt me as well. "Mr Plank," he said, "do you think Alice is quite well?"

I thought for a moment. "Physically, I think she is in good health," I said. "She's strong and well-formed – quite bonny, now that she's eating well and living in a good home."

"But in her head?" persisted Wilson. "Do you think she is well in her head?"

"Ah," I said. "I think Alice has had a great deal of sorrow in her life – hardship too." I thought back to when I had found her, more than two years earlier, pitifully alone and about to give birth, sheltering in a yard not far from where we stood now. "And I suspect that her mind has chosen to cope with it by not thinking too deeply."

"D'you mean that she's a simpleton?" asked Wilson.

"Not for one moment do I mean that," I said sternly. "On the contrary, I think Alice knows more than most women about life and its truths. But I think she chooses not to dwell on life's harshness and prefers to think about good and happy things. Like babies. Why do you ask – I mean, why do you ask now?"

Wilson has never been good at hiding what he is feeling, and now he looked utterly miserable. "When I told Alice about Buxton, she wasn't angry about being misled herself – after all, she has George, just as Eliza promised – but she was horrified to think about what Mrs Plank has suffered."

"Martha?" I asked. "What do you mean?"

Poor Wilson looked even more stricken. "Alice was at the meeting at the vinegar yard when Mrs Plank was given the message from her mother. And she realises now that she was the one who gave Eliza all the information she needed to trick Mrs Plank into thinking it was her mother. Eliza asked her about Mrs Plank, and Alice told her, thinking she was just friendly and wanting to welcome her. And now Alice is worried that Mrs Plank will blame her." He looked at me with such sadness. "Will you talk to Mrs Plank and tell her how sorry Alice is, and that she didn't mean to do it?"

"I will, if that's what Alice wants," I said, "but I should imagine that Mrs Plank has guessed already, and forgiven already. And you can tell Alice that the message from Mrs Plank's mother – sham though it was – brought her a good deal of comfort. Now, if that's all that's been worrying you, I suggest we hurry up before we're in trouble for keeping supper waiting."

We heard them as we walked towards the back door. Before I could stop myself, I said to Wilson, "That's the most beautiful sound in the world, you know – the laughter of the woman you love." He said nothing but blushed slightly. "You'll see," I continued. "By the time you're my age, you'll be as sentimental as I am. And it certainly doesn't sound like two women who have fallen out."

We stamped our boots on the doorstep and walked into the kitchen. Sitting at the table, baby George asleep in her arms, was Alice. Martha was standing, holding the back of a chair, and taking deep breaths, her face flushed.

I hung my coat on the hook and walked over to her, kissing her on the cheek. "What are you two cackling about?" I asked.

"Cackling indeed," she said indignantly. "And it's nothing we care to share with gentlemen, is it, Alice? Apart from this little one here," she leaned down and pinched George's foot, which he wriggled in his sleep, "and he's saying nothing." She turned to the stove and lifted the pot lids one by one. "All ready, so hands washed, if you please, and babies put down."

We were a merry band that evening. Wilson sat next to Alice, the baby asleep in his blanket-lined drawer on the bench between them. I caught Martha looking softly at the three of them and she smiled sheepishly; I knew what she was thinking – what she was hoping – and she knew that I knew. Martha entertained us with stories of the foolish things the girls in her school had said and done that week, and when George woke and determinedly filled his clout with the most abominable stench, we all roared with laughter at the shocked look on his little face. At that point, Wilson and I retreated to the sitting room, leaving Martha and Alice to clear up.

When they had done so, the ladies joined us around the fire. Wilson gave up the armchair to Martha and brought in a chair from the kitchen, while Alice sat at our feet, cradling George in her lap.

Without turning to look at me, Alice spoke. "Mr Plank," she said quietly, "I received a package today. I've never had one before."

I looked at Martha and she shook her head – she knew nothing of it.

"A package?" I asked. "Who sent it?"

In response, Alice handed the baby to Wilson, who took him very easily; growing up surrounded by younger siblings had made him comfortable with babies. She went into the kitchen and came back with her package and gave it to me before settling down again on the hearth rug. She left George on Wilson's knee, looking at the flames and blinking lazily.

The package – about the size of half a brick – was wrapped in brown paper and string sealed with wax, and was unopened. It was addressed to Miss Alice Godfrey at the Blue Boar.

"Mr Atkins paid for it," said Alice, looking up at me. "He thought it must be important. I will pay him back."

I looked at the markings on it. "It's from Dublin, Alice," I said. "Do you know anyone in Dublin?"

"Dublin?" she repeated, frowning. "Where is that?"

"Ireland," said Martha.

"Who would I know in Ireland?" asked Alice, looking in wonder at Wilson. He shrugged.

"Best we open it, then," I said, taking my pen-knife from my pocket and using it to lever up the wax seal.

"Here." Martha passed me the blanket that she sometimes put over her knees if she was chilly, and I spread it across my lap and put the package on top of it. I opened the brown paper wrapping, and inside was a cloth purse and a folded letter. Alice looked at them but did not touch them.

"Shall I read the letter to you?" I asked. Alice nodded. I unfolded it. "Dear Miss Godfrey," I read aloud, "I am hoping that this finds you and the baby in good health. I know that he is in safe and loving hands, and I will think of you often, even though I will be at the ends of the earth. The enclosed is for you and the baby – I hope you will accept it with the love with which it is sent. May God bless and keep you both. Yours with affection and gratitude, Eliza Mason."

Alice gazed up at me and I handed her the letter. She turned it over to examine it carefully, and then folded it and held it against her heart.

"What is in the purse, Sam?" asked Martha quietly.

I loosened the cord and tipped the purse's contents onto the blanket. "Gold sovereigns," I said, counting them quickly with a fingertip. "Twenty-five of them."

After Alice and Wilson had left – he offering to see her back to the Blue Boar before going home himself – Martha and I set the house to rights for the night, damping down the fire, securing the doors, and making sure that the rug was back in place over the loose floorboard concealing the small cavity where we kept our valuables. Alice had been terrified at the thought of taking the money with her, and had stood over me while I showed her the hiding place and added her considerable bounty to our own small savings.

When all was done, we climbed the stairs. As was my habit, I stripped quickly and jumped into bed, still pulling my nightshirt on over my head, so that I could watch my wife's more lengthy night-time preparations.

"I thought perhaps you would tire of staring at me," she said as she sat with her back to me, taking the pins from her hair. "I'm not the young woman I was," she added.

"Aye, that's true," I said. She turned to look at me and opened her mouth to object. "But that young woman was just a pencil drawing," I said, "a hint of what was to come. This, now," I held out my arms and she walked into them. "This, now: this is the masterpiece."

CHAPTER THIRTY-EIGHT

Murder will be murder

THURSDAY 20TH NOVEMBER 1828

The next morning at breakfast, Martha yawned widely as she poured my tea.

"And well you might be tired," I said, "making all those demands on me last night. I shall go to work a mere husk of a man."

Martha turned to the stove. "What nonsense you do talk," she said, but I could see from the curve of her face that she was smiling. She brought my plate over and put it in front of me and then turned her attention to my boots, which were standing by the back door. "Those need a good polish," she said. "You know how William takes notice of everything you do, so you can't let standards slip. He'd follow you to the ends of the earth, that boy."

I paused, a forkful of food halfway to my mouth. "What did you say, Mar?" I asked.

She turned to look at me, hands on her hips. "What – about your boots needing polishing?"

"No, after that," I replied. "About Wilson following me..."

"To the ends of the earth," she finished. "It was in Alice's letter last night – I liked the sound of it."

"Australia?" said Conant. "That's where you think they've gone?"

I nodded. "Eliza used the same words twice: once when she was speaking to me in the physic garden, and then again in her letter to Alice. She said she'd follow Buxton to the ends of the earth, and then she wrote that she was going to the ends of the earth. Eliza sent her package from Dublin. I checked the shipping lists in the newspaper, and ships sail regularly from Dublin to Australia – to both Sydney Cove in New South Wales, and Van Diemen's Land."

"Convict ships, you mean?" asked the magistrate.

"Aye," I said, "but they always take passengers as well. If you can pay, they'll take you – and we know that Eliza can pay."

"Indeed," said Conant. "If she can spare twenty-five sovereigns, she must have plenty more."

I nodded. "When Constable Wilson and I went to North Street, everything that Francis Buxton had stored in that back room was gone. Every last purse, every last coin, every last jewel. It was probably her plan all along, to do away with Buxton and take the lot. She must have gone there almost immediately afterwards; after all, we were there only a day later." I shook my head. "She outwitted us all."

Conant stared at me. "Are you saying that you think Eliza stabbed Francis Buxton?"

I nodded. "Constable Wilson and I have compared our recollections of what happened at the bathing pool, and we agree that John Buxton had nothing in his hands when he led his brother into the water. And his hands were on his brother's shoulders throughout the baptism – either pushing him into the water or raising him from it. He had no chance to retrieve a knife without us seeing. But Eliza, we were not watching her. When John pulled Francis from the water for the third time, he looked over his shoulder at Eliza and that's when she jumped into the pool. We assumed – everyone there assumed – that Francis was drowning and John was calling Eliza to help him. But maybe she calculated that creating confusion and the splashing of the water would give her the perfect opportunity to push the knife into Francis's back."

"A woman?" asked Conant. "With the strength to do that?"

"A woman fuelled by anger and a desire for revenge," I reminded him. "And a very slim blade. Much easier than a normal knife to slip in – and out again. And conceal in her skirts, or under John's coat, or just drop into the water."

"The weaker sex indeed," said Conant grimly.

"I think it unlikely that Miss Mason will still be in Dublin," I said, "but we must try. Might I ask you to write to the harbourmaster in Dublin, enquiring about ships leaving for Australia? Alice's package was marked as being sent on the 15th of November – Saturday last – so we can be sure Eliza was still in Dublin then."

The magistrate nodded. "In the circumstances, I think it the best we can do. But we'll not catch her, Sam: my letter will take two days to reach Dublin, and their reply the same – she'll be long gone."

"She will – but in a ship bound for a penal colony," I replied. "They have courts and judges in Australia, I believe," the magistrate nodded, "and murder will be murder even at the ends of the earth."

CHAPTER THIRTY-NINE

Wilson's plans

THURSDAY 27TH NOVEMBER 1828

Mr Conant was right about the time it would take, and it was a week later when he summoned me to his rooms to show me the reply he had received from Dublin. He was writing on a pile of papers at his table, and indicated the letter he had put to one side for me.

"One mystery is solved for us, Sam," he said. "Sit – read." And he returned to his work.

I took a seat at the table and read the letter. It had been written by a John Slater, secretary in the Ballast Office in Dublin. "Sir," it began, "I acknowledge receipt of yours of the 20th inst. I have checked our shipping lists for the period specified and can confirm that the vessel Fergusson left Dublin on the 16th inst, bound for Sydney Cove in New South Wales. On board, excepting the crew and the guards, were 217 male prisoners and 12 passengers. Among the latter there were only two women: Mrs Wentworth, the wife of the captain of the guards, and Mrs Francis, who was travelling with her husband John Francis, a merchant. I can confirm that there was no Miss Eliza Mason on board. I remain your servant."

"Eliza and John Buxton have gone together," said Wilson, shaking his head. "Calling themselves Mr and Mrs John Francis."

"It looks that way," I said, putting on my coat and handing his to Wilson.

He put it on in a distracted manner. "But that can't be an end of it," he said. "What did Mr Conant say?"

We walked out through the front office, calling farewell to Tom Neale, and walked down the steps of the police office. "He will write to the man in charge in New South Wales – the governor, I believe," I said, "giving him the details of the situation and requesting that Eliza Mason and John Buxton be arrested and charged with murder, and put before the judge." We turned into Blenheim Street. "But his letter will arrive at least a fortnight after they do, and by then they could be anywhere. With their fortune, they can buy anything – and anyone – they want."

"You think it unlikely that they will be found," Wilson said flatly as we climbed the steps to Oxford Street.

I paused to wait for a gap in the traffic. "Human nature may well betray them," I said. "As I surely do not need to remind you, those who break the law once will often do it again. They may travel to the ends of the earth, but they are still Eliza Mason and John Buxton – a man's character does not change with his location." We trotted across the road and ducked into Market Street. "And it does mean that we can reassure Alice about George – we can tell her that Eliza is not going to return to reclaim him."

"Now that you have mentioned Alice, sir," said Wilson, "I wonder whether I could have a word with you. Perhaps," he looked around him, "in here." He indicated the Cape of Good Hope. "My treat."

"In that case," I said, "how can I refuse?"

Wilson found us a quiet table in the back room of the tavern and brought over two tankards. He took a deep drink from his own and put the tankard down, then picked it up again and took another swig. He finally put it down and wiped his hand across his mouth before sitting up straight and looking me in the eye.

"Constable Plank," he said formally, "I have a mind to ask Alice to become my wife."

"Indeed," I said, enjoying my own drink with something of a clear conscience; Martha would comment on the smell on my breath, but I knew that Wilson's news would soon make her forget her disapproval.

"I'm due a pay rise at the end of the year," Wilson continued. "An old fellow in the same building where I live died last week, and my mother knows the landlord, and he has agreed that I can take on the old boy's rooms. It's not grand but it's a start. I've done my sums," he reached into his pocket and pulled out a tatty piece of paper covered with numbers and crossings out, which he passed over the table to me, "and we have enough. I went to see Mr Atkins, and he said that they can pay Alice a bit more if she's not living in with them, so she can still help with the children and all that. So with my pay rise..." His voice tailed off and he looked at me as I read his calculations.

"And how will your mother manage?" I asked.

"She's very fond of Alice," he replied. "And she knows that I want a family of my own. Now that Sally's bringing in more money from her sewing, and with Janey starting out at the same place, they have enough between them."

I passed the paper back to Wilson and he folded it carefully and put it into his pocket. "You have certainly worked out the practical side of things," I said. "But have you thought carefully enough about whether Alice is the right wife for you?"

Wilson frowned. "Do you think she is not?" he asked.

"Alice," I began carefully, leaning forward, "has had a great deal of sadness in her life."

"I know," said Wilson stoutly.

I held up my hand to silence him. "And this means," I continued, "that she may need more... protection, more sheltering than other women. She will come to rely on you, lad. You will need to be the strong one in your marriage." He opened his mouth to speak but I held up my hand again. "And at your age, you feel strong. You think that nothing can beat you. But life can be harsh and unforgiving, and when you are my age – many, many years from now – you may well not feel quite so strong. Quite so invincible. You need to imagine not only what you will be like years from now, but also what Alice will be like. And George."

Wilson said nothing. He glanced down into his empty tankard.

"Another?" I asked. He shook his head.

"I have thought about it, you know," he said softly. "I have watched you and Mrs Plank for several years, and I see how you are together. And I know myself too. When Alice looks up at me, and when little Martha held out her hands to me, and now that George quiets when he is in my arms – I know then why God made me tall and strong. I am made that way to look after others who cannot look after themselves. And I am proud and glad to do it."

"In that case, lad," I said, "we had better head home and tell Mrs Plank of your plans. She has been longing to be proved right about this."

CHAPTER FORTY

From one father to another

FRIDAY 28TH NOVEMBER 1828

I woke in the early hours of the morning, before dawn. Martha was asleep beside me, and I fancied I could see her lips still curled in a smile. When Wilson had told her of his intention the evening before, she had clasped him in a fierce hug and looked triumphantly at me. Unlike me, she had been certain from the start that they belonged together, Wilson and Alice.

"Some men need to be needed, Sam," she had said as we readied ourselves for bed. "William is one such, and by needing him, Alice will make sure that he becomes the best man he can possibly be."

And it seemed that she was not the only one who thought this. I do not have dreams very often – or, if I do, they are forgotten by the time I open my eyes – but this night was different. I had dreamt I was talking to my father, and every word of it had stayed with me on waking. He had died more than thirty years ago, but he appeared to me that night clear in every detail, sitting alongside me by my own fire.

"And so now you too know how it is to see a lad out into the world," he said, an amused look on his face. "Setting up his own home, taking on a wife and child."

"Wilson is not my son," I protested.

"Not by blood, perhaps," said my father, "no more than George is William's son by blood. But do you think he will love that boy any the less for it?" I shook my head. "And gruff though you may be – and I know why you are – William is not just your junior constable." He said it with certainty. "When he wanted to marry, where did he turn for permission?" I said nothing. "To you, Samuel." He stopped and looked into the flames for a long minute. "You and that pretty wife of yours grieve that you have no children. But you are wrong, both of you. You are surrounded by young people who have chosen you. If I had lived to your grand old age," and he winked at me, "I would be proud to be the father you are."

Martha stirred beside me. "Are you awake, Sam?" she asked sleepily. "Are you unwell? Too much ale?"

I turned to face her. "I may have been wrong, my dear," I said, "about the dead sending us messages." And I told her about my father.

Glossary

Abbess – the madam of a brothel

Bartholomew Fair – a four-day fair opened on 3rd September every year, and covering four parishes in the Smithfield area of London

Bawd – a female procuress, the madam of a bawdy house

Bird-witted – gullible and easily fooled

Bluecoat boys – pupils from charity schools, whose uniform often consisted of a blue coat (blue being the traditional colour of charity)

Bow Street runners – London's first professional police force, originally consisting of six men and operating out of Bow Street magistrates' office. Their role was gradually taken over by magistrates' constables – like Sam – and by 1828 they were spending most of their time using their city-honed skills to investigate offences outside London. The runners were formally disbanded in 1839.

Cast up one's account – to vomit

Chit – a baby or young infant

Clout – baby's nappy or diaper

Covent Garden nun – a prostitute working in or near Covent Garden

Cracksman – a housebreaker, a burglar

Cropsick – sick to the stomach from drunkenness

Dead men – empty bottles and glasses, as found on the table of a drinking establishment

Dry boots – a sly, humorous fellow

Fart catcher – a valet or footman, who always walks behind his master or mistress

File – see "Old file"

Grease someone in the fist – to bribe someone

Greenhead – an inexperienced young man

Gull – a simple, credulous person who is easily deceived

Hackney coach – a vehicle for hire, with four wheels, two horses and six seats, driven by a jarvey

Hum box – pulpit

Jarvey – a driver of a hackney coach

Ken – a house in general, but more usually a house where thieves and rogues meet

Light-heeled – swift at running

Molly house – a brothel for homosexual men, where male prostitutes – and customers – may dress as women, and "marriages" may be performed

Nip – a half-pint

Nose – a criminal who informs or turns King's evidence in hope of a lighter sentence

Old file – someone with long and successful experience as an adept fraudster

Old Harry – the Devil

Primitives – a group of Methodists, active in England in the nineteenth century, devoted to practising a purer form of their religion, which was closer to the earliest Methodism and distinct from Wesleyan Methodism, from which they had split

Quality – the upper class of society

Queer plunger – a cheat who pretends to drown in order that an accomplice can rescue and revive him and thus claim a reward from the Royal Humane Society

Ranters – a pejorative term for Primitive Methodists

Rookery – city slum area frequented by criminals and prostitutes

Threepenny ordinary – a set meal of meat, broth and beer, costing threepence

Toper – a drunkard

Topping man – a wealthy man

Shanks' pony – one's own legs, used as a means of transport

Trim – to cheat or deceive someone, especially of money

Waterman – originally watermen plied boats for hire on the Thames, but as hackney coaches took over as the main means of public transport in London, a compromise was reached to employ former watermen on coach stands around the city to provide water and care to the horses pulling the coaches – this is the role they fulfil in the 1820s

Thank you for reading this book. If you liked what you read, please would you leave a short review on the site where you purchased it, or recommend it to others? Reviews and recommendations are not only the highest compliment you can pay to an author; they also help other readers to make more informed choices about purchasing books.

ABOUT THE AUTHOR

Susan Grossey graduated from Cambridge University in 1987 and since then has made her living from crime. She advises financial institutions and others on money laundering – how to spot criminal money, and what to do about it. She has written many non-fiction books on the subject of money laundering, as well as contributing monthly articles to the leading trade magazine and maintaining a popular anti-money laundering blog.

Her first work of fiction was the inaugural book in the Sam Plank series, "Fatal Forgery". "The Man in the Canary Waistcoat" was her second novel, "Worm in the Blossom" her third, "Portraits of Pretence" her fourth, and now "Faith, Hope and Trickery" is her fifth. Two more Sam Plank mysteries are planned, to complete the series of seven.

Printed in Great Britain
by Amazon